BITTER SEEDS

Christina Green

Chivers Press   •   G.K. Hall & Co.
Bath, Avon, England   Thorndike, Maine USA

This Large Print edition is published by Chivers Press, England, and by G.K. Hall & Co., USA.

Published in 1997 in the U.K. by arrangement with the author.

Published in 1997 in the U.S. by arrangement with Dorian Literary Agency.

U.K. Hardcover ISBN 0–7451–6948–1 (Chivers Large Print)
U.K. Softcover   ISBN 0–7451–6960–0 (Camden Large Print)
U.S. Softcover   ISBN 0–7838–1941–2 (Nightingale Collection Edition)

The text of this Large Print edition is unabridged.
Other aspects of the book may vary from the original edition.

Set in 16 pt. New Times Roman.

Printed in Great Britain on acid-free paper.

British Library Cataloguing in Publication Data available

Library of Congress Cataloging-in-Publication Data

Green, Christina.
  Bitter seeds / by Christina Green.
    p. cm.
  ISBN 0–7838–1941–2 (lg print : sc)
  1. Large type books. I. Title.
[PR6057.R3378B58 1997]
823′.914—dc20

96–30933

CHAPTER ONE

Freddie Freeman brought his mud-stained old Morris Traveller to a wheezing halt outside the cemetery gates. 'Want me to come in with you, love?'

'No, thanks, I can manage.' Anna Hoskins got out, clutching the bunch of Sweet Williams she'd just picked from the front garden of Greenways farmhouse. 'I won't be long.'

She turned into the drive, ignoring Freddie's dog-like gaze and feeling unexpectedly irritated. It was good to have a friend, of course, but she wasn't the first woman in the world to suddenly lose her husband after a massive heart attack and she wouldn't be the last. Life had to go on, didn't it? And she had a lot to be thankful for; the security of her own home, her good health, and a sensible, down-to-earth philosophy of life. She wasn't one to sit and cry over spilt milk. She'd get by all right.

But once she had reached the newly-mounded grave and put the flowers into a jar brought for the purpose, something deep inside her stirred and she just stood there, frighteningly aware that everything had changed. Ray was gone and there was that uneasy feeling back again—the uneasiness she had felt after that woman had mentioned knowing Ray

Remorselessly, her mind slipped back to last Friday week, the day of the funeral. The hard, bright sunlight had shone down with overpowering heat that had seemed to shrivel her as she stood there, tearless and stoic, watching the first spadefuls of earth rattle down over the coffin. Friends and neighbours had been a great support to her, and, of course, Freddie had been a tower of strength.

'Come on, old girl—time to leave now.' His low voice had kept on at her to go when the service ended, but something had made her pause, strangely undecided what to do next.

'In a minute, Freddie,' she'd said sharply, nudging his arm. 'You go on. I'm all right. I'll come when I'm ready.' And, obedient as ever, he'd left her alone by the grave.

But not quite alone, for someone else had stayed behind. Anna lifted her head, staring across at a woman who looked back at her with a curious, slightly-embarrassed expression.

Who was this stranger? A woman younger than herself, plump and pretty, flaunting her femininity in a swirling-skirted dress of navy-blue shiny material, with discreet touches of white at the neck and wrist, the becoming hat a matching straw that dipped over bleached hair and anxious, heavily made-up eyes.

The woman smiled nervously as she met Anna's candid gaze. 'You have my sympathy, Mrs Hoskins,' she said in a low voice.

Anna smiled stiffly. 'Thank you.' Her

2

emotions, held in check during the ordeal of the long afternoon, were beginning to fray. 'Did you know my husband, Mrs—er—Mrs—?'

'Leach. Gilly Leach.' Again that fleeting smile, the brown eyes falling and avoiding Anna's, as she added, 'Yes, indeed, I did. Ray was very kind to me after my own husband died. He was a wonderful man...' The halting words fell into a silence taut with awkwardness.

Anna felt rather uneasy, but was unable to find any rational reason for it. Ray had known many people who had remained just names to her; he was a generous, outgoing man, while she thought only of her family and farm. Now she narrowed her eyes as she stared at Gilly Leach, seeing as she did so an odd, knowing expression flit across the cast-down brown eyes.

Because of her uneasiness, Anna hardened. Why should she feel so apprehensive, because of the way this soft and ingratiating woman opposite had said she knew Ray? Gilly Leach. Anna's lip curled. Now there was a stupid name, foolish and fussy. It suited its owner. The thought gave comfort, but then, out of the blue came an uncomfortable memory, even as she regarded Gilly Leach with scorn. He'd had his secrets, had Ray...

Over the grave a movement caught Anna's disapproving gaze again—Gilly Leach's hands

3

fluttering as if she didn't know what to do with them. All white and soft and useless, like the woman they belonged to. Unconsciously, Anna drew her five-feet-three inches to a greater height, reminding herself of her strength and competency as she did so. Ever since she'd persuaded Ray to move back into the old family farmhouse when Auntie May died, over twenty years ago, and they'd gone self-sufficient, she'd taken over many of the tasks that a man normally did.

Ray had been good with motors and tractors, but he hadn't known a thing about growing plants. She'd had to learn all that for both of them. It hadn't been hard, because she'd grown up on this land; it was like coming home when they moved into Greenways Farm all that time ago.

Now she glanced down at her own hands, safely hidden in sensible cotton gloves that matched the dark-grey jacket and skirt she wore. She knew they were hard and useful. She felt them help towards gaining a welcome superiority over this insipid stranger who, even now, was backing away with an apologetic last smile.

Anna sighed. There was no one on the other side of the grave now. Just the relentless sunlight, shafting down.

The cloying scent of flowers rising from the piled wreaths that lay close by, assailed her with nostalgia. A stupidly, inconsequential

4

thought that this sun was good for the strawberries drifted across her bewildered mind. And then agony, sharp and dark, making her tremble as she stood there with the truth hitting her bleakly, she was alone, and Ray had gone.

*　　　*　　　*

Now it was time to go, to join Freddie and the few chosen friends who were invited to return to the farm and share the good, wholesome food that she'd left ready. Her own bread, farm vegetables and salad, washed down with Ray's precious home-made country wines. The parsley had been his favourite.

Anna stared around her, touched suddenly with an unfamiliar sense of panic. She felt so terribly alone ... but there must be someone, somewhere, in this hour of need? Then Freddie's voice called through the silence and she turned, leaving the grave behind, forgotten, as she went rapidly back to the waiting car and Freddie's affectionate smile.

'Come on, love,' he said, and the familiar word helped her to gather up the loose threads of self-control, so frighteningly about to slip out of her grasp.

'What are you in such a hurry for?' Her voice sounded sharp and far away, but she was grateful to him. It was never easy for her to show her feelings, but Freddie understood.

5

The awful moment had passed and now she was her own woman again. She got into the car, looking straight ahead as Freddie started the car. There would be other times for returning and remembering Ray. Right now she needed to go home, to be among her own things and friends. Back in the world that had, just for a crazy moment, tilted almost upside down.

The long, hot afternoon lingered endlessly as comfortable voices chatted quietly in the parlour, where the tea had been laid out, and she sat on a hard, over-upholstered chair which she had never liked, listening to the hum of conversation filling the old-fashioned room.

When, finally, the neighbours and friends rose to leave, Anna saw them to the door. Mrs Hicks, from Well Farm in the village, nodded at her kindly. 'I'll be off now, my dear. A lovely meal. I hope as you'll soon feel better ... Any time you want to pop around and see us ... Well, we're always there.'

The wheezy voice, full of sympathy, unexpectedly penetrated Anna's failing defences, and all she could say was a muttered, 'Thank you, Mrs Hicks. I'll remember that.'

One by one the visitors departed, their subdued voices echoing in the quiet afternoon air until the gate clicked and only Pete Lazenby remained in the room.

Anna thought wryly that he looked out of place in his slightly thread-bare suit. He stood by the door, listening and watching, as he'd done all afternoon. Now he grinned at her and shifted from one large foot to the other, nodding emphatically as if to assure her that everything would soon be back to normal.

'Strawberries'll be ready to pick soon if this sun goes on, Mrs Hoskins.'

She watched the young man stuff earth-engrained hands into tight pockets, clearly not knowing what else to do with them. The flavour of the soil he tended lay about him, regardless of the shining cleanliness of his white shirt and the newly-plastered-down, dark hair.

She felt herself begin to relax again as he smiled down at her. 'Yes, Pete, you're right. Just what we need. We'll be picking by next week-end, I should think.' Now she could shut away the trappings of death, forget the funeral, and Gilly Leach, instead visualise punnets of large, juicy berries, piled up and ready for delivery to the restaurant with whom she'd signed a contract earlier in the year. She could smell them, fragrant and mouth-watering. A feeling of immense achievement suddenly filled her, and for a moment life was good again.

Pete shuffled again. 'Better get back to the hoeing...' He'd had enough, and she didn't blame him. It was good of him to have come, but he'd worked for her for the last eleven years and was one of the old school, reliable, supportive, and conscientious.

7

Whatever Pete had thought of Ray's non-ability as a smallholder, he'd come to his funeral, tight suit and all. Anna found herself moved enough to reach out and touch his arm. 'Thanks, Pete. I'm so glad you came.'

Surprise lit both their faces, for never before had she shown such emotion. She was his employer, fair, friendly, and knowledgeable, and there it had stopped. Now, abruptly, the relationship had grown.

Pete stepped away very quickly, still nodding. 'That's all right, Mrs Hoskins. See you later, then—'

He disappeared, and Anna stared at the door, wondering at her uncharacteristic emotional outburst, but after the loneliness of the afternoon's ordeal it had been good to know that Pete was there. Bashful, anxious to get back to work—but there.

When the old house was again empty, the echoes of the visitors' voices fading with the lengthening shadows, Anna went into the cosy little sitting-room which she and Ray had always used in preference to the big parlour. Their chairs stood on each side of the open fireplace, with last week's papers still piled high between them. Everything had happened so fast that she'd had no time to move them.

Now her heart sank, but she went forward determinedly. Personal effects must be sorted out, and it was far better to have the task behind her than lingering on, like a sad ghost.

Yes, she would go through Ray's bits and pieces this evening, and then it would be all finished.

Books, papers, some photographs, records and magazines soon found their way into suitable homes. Then she turned to the desk that stood against the opposite wall. A tidy man, Ray had dealt with important matters as they cropped up. There was little in the desk that gave her any concern. Bills had been paid, the copy of his will was there, together with papers concerning car insurance and so on. Yes, all was in order.

She sighed with relief. It hadn't been so bad, after all. Once the job was finished she would make a cup of coffee and sit down quietly to relax her churning mind before going up to bed. Just this last drawer to empty and go through.

*   *   *

And then she saw it, tucked beneath a small pile of maps, a folded letter with a scribbled, familiar name showing at the end of it. *Gilly.* It was written in a scrappy, uneven hand, so reminiscent of the frail personality she had met earlier this very afternoon. Fascinated, yet appalled, Anna opened the letter and read it through, feeling again as she did so that stab of uneasiness that Gilly Leach had first engendered in her. But now the uneasiness was

9

developing into rage, disbelief and bitterness.

'I'll never forget you, my dear, and I can only hope that you feel the same about me. Those few months we shared gave me new hope and confidence when I was so unhappy. Dear Ray, I know I shall always go on loving you, even though we can't—'

Anna didn't bother to read the rest of it. Enough was enough. With her legs abruptly turned to jelly, she sank down into the nearest chair. Suspicion had become hard fact, and her whole world was falling apart.

At first she tried to fight it. Ray and that woman ... But it was impossible, surely? He could never have been unfaithful! It wasn't true. It couldn't be! Anna shouted silently to herself. They hadn't had the most blissful of marriages—well, who did? But they'd stayed together. That was the one thing that had kept her going after the numbing shock of his death, the knowledge that they'd shared a good marriage.

And now this ghastly news that the marriage had been based on deceit. Suddenly their life together had turned into a false and unreal relationship, a nightmare instead of a pleasantly remembered dream. Anna stared at the letter again and knew, finally, that it was the truth. Otherwise why had Gilly Leach bothered to write to him? And why had Ray—so neat and orderly in all his doings—cared enough to hoard the letter as he had

10

done? Anna saw again Gilly Leach's face across his grave and knew then, with a horrible certainty, that Ray and Gilly had been lovers.

The pain was almost too much to bear. She blinked fiercely, spurning the weak tears. She caught her breath as undeniable knowledge swept in, and she forced herself to face it. So Ray had actually preferred another woman to her—that fussy, over-dressed, insipid creature called Gilly Leach.

It was unbearable to have to accept that she, reliable and competent, running her smallholding with one hand and coping with her gentle, idle husband with the other; who never needed help, not at work nor at play; was the woman who now shook and choked back sobs as she realised that the foundations of the marriage she had regarded as strong and enduring had, in fact, turned out to be based on lies and deceit.

It was very late when, at last, she left the room and went wearily up to bed, her mind numb with misery and her body aching with tiredness; alone in the too-large bed, she lay wide awake, wondering how she would be able to continue her life, now that her peace of mind and happiness was shattered, seemingly for ever.

*   *   *

The first few weeks were the hardest, Anna

discovered, once the funeral was behind her and life continued on its way. She found her initial determination to carry on gradually weakening as the days passed. Gilly Leach's face was always there when she shut her eyes at night, and that whispering voice haunted her dreams.

One hazy morning in early June she rose early, because the double bed painfully emphasised Ray's absence, and she could hardly wait to get outside, into the healing atmosphere of things growing in the garden and surrounding fields. The heatwave had continued and now the first picking of strawberries was already safely delivered in the old van that Ray had just finished servicing, the day before he died.

Anna, arriving back from taking the fruit to the Keeper's Cottage Restaurant, two miles down the road from the farm, suddenly stopped in her tracks, staring at the dark-green van over which Ray had spent so much time. She could see him, quite distinctly, coming into the kitchen to wash his hands and tidy up, saying that the job was done.

'OK for another three thousand miles, my love.' He'd thrown her a grin as she stood by the stove, getting tea ready. Hot ham and pineapple, Anna recalled now. The smell was all about her. And she remembered, too, what she'd thought at that moment, He may be hopeless at growing things, but give him any

12

sort of motor and he's a miracle-worker.

'That'll get you to Keeper's safely when the strawberries are ripe. And for the next six months. After that, well, we'll see...'

They'd been discussing investing in a new van, but he'd talked her out of it, saying he'd patch up the old one for a while longer. And he had.

Almost as if he'd known, Anna thought wonderingly now.

She banged shut the double doors, gave the van a little pat of gratitude, and, sighing, went towards the farthest field where Pete was at the endless task of hoeing, thinking hard as she did so.

Employing Pete had been an indulgence that they really couldn't afford.

'Four miserable acres and three people working it?' Ray had scoffed eleven years ago. 'That's not a viable proposition, my darling. You must be mad!'

Mad, or just plain soft, she had insisted. For how could anyone turn away a homeless, vulnerable adolescent who'd just landed on the doorstep?

Reaching the field gate, Anna stopped and leaned upon it, feeling the heat of the midday sun burning her bare shoulders beneath the sleeveless T-shirt. She watched Pete's lean figure moving in a graceful, effortless pattern as he went slowly down the rows of young vegetables.

13

He'd been just seventeen when he arrived at Greenway Farm, directed there by old PC Walker, who used to play bar billiards with Ray at the Pig and Whistle.

'I went to the police station and asked if they knew of any jobs going,' Pete explained as he stood, embarrassed and wet through with the sleeting November rain, at the back door of the farm. 'The chap there said you might have one...'

His lean face, still spotty with adolescence, and his worried, yet direct, gaze, had touched Anna's usually unassailable heart. Perhaps because he reminded her of the son who had never grown beyond four months old—the baby, Harry, who had suffered an inexplicable cot death, and who now was just a bitter-sweet memory in the background of her busy life.

Of course, she had offered Pete a job, taken him into the kitchen to dry off, fed him, and then bulldozed a reluctant Ray into agreeing that they really did need help if the old cottage by the gate was to be made habitable and an extra source of revenue. Not that it had earned a penny piece as a result; Anna's plans of a holiday cottage and long lets faded when she saw how easily and gratefully young Pete Lazenby made it into a home.

'Something I always dreamed of, having a home of my own, all the time I was at Barnardo's,' he'd confided in her, face glowing with pleasure as he lugged rotting timbers and

14

window-frames out of the ruin and assisted Ray in making the old place habitable again.

An orphan dumped by an uncaring mother, his father unknown, Pete had, over the years he spent working at Greenways Farm, become a surrogate son to Ray and Anna, although she personally would never have dreamed of admitting it. What Ray thought, she didn't know. It was a subject they avoided discussing.

So Pete became the general help and was given a pittance of weekly pocket money, his board and lodging being taken to balance the hours he spent working on the smallholding, helping Ray with the cars for repair that littered the yard, and eventually becoming an integral part of Greenways Farm.

Anna, still leaning on the gate, was engulfed in another surge of emotion as her thoughts wandered the mazes of memory. She'd taken Pete for granted all these years. After that one brief spasm of feeling when he first appeared, she'd gone on to think of him simply as another mouth to feed, more washing on a Monday, and a strong body who would run errands for her. Now she found herself wondering at the life he led. Was he content? Did he have any friends? Would he stay here for ever? Will he want to marry, one day? The last question echoed around her mind as she unlatched the gate and went across the field towards him, realising with a pang, that he was a complete stranger.

'Pete...'

He was so immersed in his work that at first he didn't hear her. She called again, and he looked up, his blank expression resolving at once into the usual cheery smile. For no reason at all, something clutched at Anna's heart strings. He was good-looking and mature now—another thing she hadn't noticed before. There was honesty in that straight gaze, and humour about the up-curving mouth. Why couldn't she have had a son like this?

The painful thought came like the piercing of a sword, making her own smile crumble, forcing her to turn, to bend and examine the row of young carrots as if her life depended on it. For no one, and certainly not Pete, must ever see how bereft she was these days, how empty her life without Ray, how frightening the future that stretched so bleakly ahead.

'No carrot fly yet?' She fingered the bright, fringed leaves and kept her face hidden until self-control returned.

Pete's calm voice sounded the epitome of contentment, and spread reassuringly into her own depressed mind. 'Not a sign,' he said. 'Reckon we've got it beat this year.'

'Good.' Now she was able to straighten up, to smile at him and meet that steady gaze. 'Don't work too hard, Pete, this sun's a killer. Come and have a drink, if you like. I'll make some fresh lemonade.'

She noticed his look of amazement and

thought wryly that no doubt he wondered what had come over her. Never before had she thought to give such an invitation.

'Well, thanks—I'll just finish this row.'

Anna felt his eyes still on her as she returned to the house, but didn't care what he thought. It seemed that every day was bringing a new lesson in living to her; today she realised, suddenly and urgently, that you never miss people until they're gone. Ray had gone, and she hadn't appreciated him properly. She wasn't going to let that happen with Pete.

*   *   *

Or with Freddie...

During the afternoon she made a point of walking the two-hundred-odd yards down the narrow country lane to Freddie's bungalow, wondering as she went about the reception she'd get. Freddie usually came to her, never she to him, so this was quite a momentous occasion.

As she expected, he was very surprised to see her. 'Anna! What on earth—something wrong, love?' He left the easel in the corner of the straggling, overgrown garden, a small, chubby man in slap-happy clothes with wispy brown hair and open-toed sandals proclaiming his Bohemian attitudes, and came to her side as she paused, just inside the gate.

'Of course not. Why should there be?' she

countered smoothly. 'Just thought it was high time I paid you a social call. After all, you've been on at me for ages to come and see your latest paintings.'

'Well, it's lovely to have you here.' The usual, wide grin spread all over his face. 'Come in, old girl, and see what you think.'

Indoors, the bungalow was as arty and crafty as Freddie himself. Examples of his work hung on every wall and shelves overflowed with pottery, photographs, sculptures, and general bric-à-brac of every period. Anna looked about her, slightly bemused. She had thought her own home far from tidy, but this was really something more. But, of course, Freddie was an artist of considerable talent and so must be excused.

Luckily, he was too busy extolling the abstract mural he had recently painted around the kitchen walls to be aware of her reaction to his home.

'Straight lines,' he burbled happily, standing back and looking affectionately at the brilliant conglomeration of colours and shapes that seemed to fill the small room. 'The essence of this particular three-dimensional pattern, and I've caught it exactly, don't you think? Eh, old girl?'

Spinning around with his customary fleetness of foot, he confronted her, bright grin fading as he saw the expression on her face. 'Ah—you don't like it...'

He sounded so much like a small boy refused his favourite toy that Anna hastily reconsidered her verdict. Until just recently, she would have stuck to her guns and said flatly that he was, no doubt, very clever, but it wasn't her sort of thing, and that she preferred a pretty, old-fashioned picture, not a great long daub of smudgy lines. Now, however, something in his spaniel eyes touched her, and she knew she was unable to hurt him by coming out with the truth.

'It's certainly—er—spectacular, Freddie.' That, at least, was true. She saw his face lose its pleading expression and pride returned.

'Good, good! But do you like it—eh?'

She sought desperately for words, and after a moment's hesitation surprised herself by saying tactfully, 'Right now it's a bit beyond me, but who knows? I might grow into it, Freddie.'

His grin overflowed again, and briskly he went to fill the kettle and put it on the stove. 'Cup of tea? To celebrate?'

She was uncertain whether the celebration was in honour of the newly-painted wall or of her visit, but merely nodded amiably, went back to the sitting-room, and sat down in the corner of the sagging studio couch that leaned against the wall below the window.

It seemed that she had developed new eyes just lately. Things long familiar had, strangely, become different—fresher and more interesting. At first, she had thought that the summer sunshine, so bright and encouraging, had enlivened her horizons. But now, several weeks after Ray's funeral, she knew better. Her life had expanded.

She was seeing everything clearer, experiencing deeper feelings, even understanding people better. She supposed that it was because she had been forced to look into her own life with such painfully probing clarity after finding out about Ray and Gilly Leach.

It had been, and still was, a hard, embittering experience. But it had taught her some lessons; Anna neither cared nor worried, now, about how she would get on with her life. Already she had learned merely to tackle each day as it came. Each task. Each thought.

But today, happily, for the first time, she sensed a benefit from her deeper understanding of things. Now she was able to look at Freddie's home and see that it was a cosy reflection of his own nature, not just a mishmash of untidiness created by an easy-going artist. The bungalow demonstrated his placid manner with the world in general, his fascination for all things beautiful and well-crafted—and essentially, his niceness.

When he came in with a tray of slopping tea, she accepted her mug with a grateful smile, making no acid comment on the drips that fell in her lap. She was beginning to understand that it was important to accept people, not to automatically revile them because they were different.

Freddie sat beside her, happily drinking with huge, enjoyable gulps. Anna smelled turpentine and flower fragrance and turned to him with a smile. 'Have you been working out there in the garden, all day long?'

'Of course. Painting takes time.'

'Did you have any lunch?'

'Er—well, no—' he fidgeted uneasily and she realised, with a stab of dismay, that he was expecting to be reprimanded. The old Anna, as he knew, would have rebuked him sharply.

Instead, she said gently, 'Another time, if you're too busy to cook, or even grab a sandwich, come up to Greenway. There's usually some soup, or a salad—Pete and I are always starving after our morning's work. Don't forget, now, Freddie—'

She could have laughed aloud at the surprised expression on his chubby face, and then impulsively put a hand on his arm as he gaped at her. 'And don't look like that. I'm only trying to be friendly!'

For a moment he paused, smiling, and then said very quietly, 'Friendship is a beautiful thing, wouldn't you say?'

Anna considered. Suddenly she was thankful for the chance to tell him just what his support had meant to her. 'It certainly is, Freddie,' she answered sincerely. 'I'm grateful for yours; you've been such a help since—since Ray went. I don't know how I'd have managed on my own.'

Freddie bowed his head, and then, as if he'd suddenly come to a decision, looked very intently at her. 'Anna, old girl,' he said, 'I'd do anything for you. Anything at all. Remember that, won't you?'

Something in the quiet words startled her, bringing dismay and shock. Freddie as a friend was one thing, but Freddie with a throb in his voice was another. Quickly she drank the remainder of her tea, feeling it was time to go.

But, almost as if churning waters had been undammed, he was speaking again, leaning towards her, his smile so full of genuine emotion that she hadn't the heart to stop him. 'You see, my dear—well, it's hard to put into words. But you've come to mean a lot to me. Oh, maybe I shouldn't say this, not with Ray so recently gone, but, good Lord, Anna, you must know how I feel?'

She stiffened, wanting to recoil and forget what he'd just said. A declaration of love— from Freddie? The idea was ludicrous. And then, an instant later, it was distasteful. Marriage and husbands were hardly topics she cared for at the moment. Freddie was an old and valued friend—he could never be anything more.

She sat there, staring into his pleading brown eyes, not knowing how to reply. It

22

seemed an eternity before she was finally able to say flatly, 'I didn't know. I never guessed. I mean, you and Ray and I—we've been such friends, ever since you came to live in Broadwood. Freddie, I don't want to hurt you—but—'

She stopped abruptly, sadly aware that however she phrased it, she must inevitably wound him. Already his smile had diminished, the hope in the eyes had clouded over. The smell of turpentine on his shirt suddenly overpowered Anna, and she had a foolishly-fantastic vision of marrying Freddie and having to live with that smell for ever. Harshly, she added, 'I'm sorry. I can't think of the future yet: it's too soon. And, anyway, I don't love you, Freddie...'

It was said. Holding her breath, she waited for his reaction. But there were no dramatics, no emotional scenes. He merely nodded his head in quiet acceptance and leaned back against the couch.

'Of course you don't. Why should you? I'm just a useless sort of chap who dreams romantic dreams'—the smile flashed out again—'and paints pictures you don't like! Ah, well, that's life, isn't it? But I shan't give up, you know. I'll stay around. Be your friend, like you said. And one day I'll ask you again...'

They looked at one another with new perceptions, and Anna's mind ran in circles. She hadn't suspected such hidden strength;

23

now she saw the determination in that gentle smile and felt a new aspect of respect added to the friendliness that she would always have for him. 'Thank you, Freddie.' The words slipped out without thought, and she smiled. There was a silence between them. Then he got to his feet and picked up the tray.

'More tea, old girl? Plenty in the pot.'

Anna was able to resume her usual casual manner. 'Sorry, but I really must get back. Pete'll be waiting for his meal.'

'Well, lovely to have seen you. Come again, eh?' At the garden gate he nodded and smiled, watching as she went down the lane, heading back for the farm.

For once, Anna didn't notice the sun on her back, or the birds singing in the hedges beside her, as she went briskly back to Greenways, for her mind was still confused with Freddie's surprising declaration. Freddie in love? She had never thought of him as a man who needed a woman. He had his home, his art, and a wide circle of friends, both locally and in London, where he came from. She'd always imagined him to be content.

And yet—bitterness spread through her—how little one ever knew of other people's inner lives. Look at Ray and Gilly Leach.

At the farm gate she turned off the road and followed the track back to the house, upset and miserable. All the optimism with which she had set out to see Freddie had gone; now she felt

24

she must keep him at a distance, friend or not. How else could she cope with his devotion?

But then she approached the garden, and the beauty of the flowers, the music of the plundering bees, and the general atmosphere of all things growing revived her slightly. After tea she would work out here alone. Maybe it would cheer her up a little.

At the back door of the farmhouse, something made her stop and turn, looking for what she didn't know. She frowned as she stared about her, and for no reason at all a feeling of uneasy apprehension began to fill her.

Pete stood at the gate of the vegetable field talking to a stranger. A girl ... As Anna stared, he saw her, nodded in her direction, and said something to the girl that made her look across at Anna.

The girl gave him a last, fleeting smile and began walking back to the house, her gait clumsy and heavy. Suddenly Anna realised she was pregnant.

As she drew nearer, her voice floated through the quietness of the late afternoon. 'Are you Mrs Hoskins? Ray Hoskins' wife?'

Anna was beginning to feel mounting apprehension. She looked at the weary young face confronting her and felt a premonition of disaster. Something awful was about to happen, and she was quite unable to prevent it. There was nowhere she could run to, no place to hide.

Speechless, she stared at the girl, taking in the advanced state of pregnancy that filled the cheap cotton skirt and bulging sun-top, noticing with distaste the lank, tangled mop of brown hair with its dead, bleached ends, and then, with growing horror as she looked into the suspicious grey-green eyes, knew that they were Ray's eyes...

'Who are you? What do you want? Why have you come here?' The questions leaped out, her voice harsh and afraid, and she knew the answers even as she spoke.

The girl leaned heavily against the door jamb and stared back at her, the face expressionless and unfriendly. 'I'm Ros Leach, and your precious husband was my dad. I've come here because my ultra-respectable mum threw me out. The baby's due in a few days, and I don't know where else to go...'

There was an unexpected catch in the flat voice, and as Anna watched, fascinated and silent, she saw tears begin to trickle down the tense, lovely young face.

Ros gulped and cupped her heavy burden with trembling hands in a protective gesture that said more to Anna than any words could. 'Can I—can I stay here? Please...'

CHAPTER TWO

Anna's head spun. She stared at the weeping girl beside her, unable to say anything for the images that filled her mind. Ray and the Leach woman together—for how long? It must have started when she and Ray moved in here, to Greenways Farm—nearly twenty years now. The girl looked about nineteen ... so it must be true, that she was their child. After all, why should she bother to make up such a tale?

Pain welled up, confusing and bitter, and Anna heard herself shouting, 'Of course you can't stay here! My husband's dead, you're nothing to me; go back to your own mother; make her take you in. She's responsible for you.'

The girl dried her eyes and pulled herself together.

'Your husband was responsible for me, too,' she said bluntly, 'And if he's gone, then I should have thought you ought to help. After all, it was probably your fault that he and she—'

'No!' Anna took a step back. 'Don't dare say that! Ray and I were happy, we had a good marriage; just because your mother got her claws into him—'

'That's not what it says in his letter.'

'What letter?'

'The one I found in Mum's writing-case the other day. The letter he wrote—yes, your husband, Ray. He said that she'd given him a happiness he never found with you; that he wished he could live with my mum in her little suburban semi; that he couldn't be happy in this old farm of yours. He said that you thought more of the farm than you did of him.'

'I don't believe it!' But Anna could no longer stop the threatening tears, for she knew she was hearing the truth.

Ray had been unsettled at the farm. She'd taken no notice at the time, but now, now ... Oh, God! Anna put her hands to her face, staring at Ros helplessly. Was that how Ray had really felt? Had she, in truth, driven him into an affair with Gilly Leach?

Sobbing, she bowed her head. 'I didn't know. Didn't realise. I never meant—'

For a moment, silence stretched between them, emphasising the hostility. There was only the sound of a blackbird in the beech tree outside, and a dog barking at the other end of the village. Then Ros's voice broke the silence suddenly, unexpectedly gentle and apologetic.

'Look, Mrs Hoskins, I'm sorry I've upset you. I only said all that because I wanted you to see that I need to stay here. I haven't got anywhere else to go.'

Anna stared with haggard eyes. 'What about the baby's father? Why can't you go to him?'

Ros's face tightened mutinously. 'Because I

28

can't. I'm better off away from him. He's—well, never mind. Look'—the pleading note crept back into her voice—'it'll only be until I have the baby. After that I'll find a job, or something. Just for a week or so, that's all. I won't be a nuisance. Oh, please...'

Abruptly, Anna's misery died, and in its place anger began to rage. This was all Ray's fault! If he hadn't been so idle and useless, he would never have befriended that wretched Leach woman, and this girl wouldn't be here now, badgering her.

She threw Ros an irritable scowl. 'No, I'm sorry, but the answer's no. Go to the local hospital, they'll take you in. That's the best place for you.'

'But...' Ros's pale face blanched even further, and her hands flew to her stomach. Her voice grew suddenly shrill. 'For God's sake, haven't you any compassion at all? Have you got a daughter of your own? Wouldn't you want another woman to help her if she was like me? Mrs Hoskins, please, help me!'

Anna said baldly, 'I haven't got any children, and I'm glad—if you're a typical example.'

They stared at one another, and Anna sensed that she had won. The girl's expression was full of hostile frustration, and the hands that had been cupping her body fell wearily to her sides. She looked beaten.

'Someone like you doesn't deserve to have
29

children!'

Anna's triumph was short-lived, and the bitter words threw her back into the past. She saw Harry again, asleep in her arms, smiling and gurgling in his cot—knew the warm, sweet smell of him, the feel of his skin against hers. 'That's a terrible thing to say,' she muttered brokenly. 'You've no right—'

A strong hand gripped her arm, and a determined voice cut across her words. 'Mrs Hoskins, don't say any more. You'll only make things worse.'

Pete Lazenby was at her side, his face unhappy. She glowered at him. 'What's it got to do with you? This girl...'

'I heard. I'm sorry, but I couldn't help hearing. I was just coming in to tea, and you didn't bother to keep your voices down. Now, look—'

Suddenly he smiled down at her, his sun-tanned face pleading, like a son asking his mother for a favour. 'She could have the cottage,' he said persuasively. 'Just for a while. Till the baby comes. I can find a bed somewhere in the village. Mrs Hoskins, you can't chuck her out; I mean, well, you'd never forgive yourself if you did anything like that, you know.'

Anna swayed, putting a hand to the wall to support herself. Pete's calm and logical words made a certain sense. Of course, she was still angry. She'd never forgive Ray and that Leach

30

woman, never—and the girl was a careless young madam, but—maybe he was right.

For a long moment she thought and thought. Then—

'All right,' she agreed reluctantly, going into the open doorway, not looking at either of the young faces that watched so anxiously. 'She can stay. For a week or so. Not in the cottage, Pete, in the spare room upstairs. There's no reason why you should have to give up your home.'

'There's every reason, Mrs Hoskins.' His quiet words made her turn to meet his eyes. 'I know what it's like to be without a home. I wouldn't want my worst enemy to go through what I did when I was younger ... so I don't mind letting her have it for as long as she needs it.'

Anna swallowed painfully. There was a hard lump in her throat and deep inside her something knotted agonisingly. Pete had put it all very plainly. He had shown her exactly how wrong she was. She must seem very hard and cruel to him, thinking as he did. And then, suddenly it was all-important that he should think well of her; Pete, who was the sort of young man Harry might have been.

She took a deep breath and looked at the girl standing there in the fading sunlight, frail despite her heavy burden, and alone. Poor thing, silly and defiant as she was!

'Come on in,' Anna said flatly. 'What's your

31

name? Rosalind, did you say? Well, you can have the spare room. I'll air the bed while you have a bath—you look worn out, it'll relax you. And then we'll have something to eat.'

* * *

The old house appeared to have taken on a new lease of life. Anna paused, taking bedding from the airing cupboard on the landing, to smell the soft perfumed fragrance of soap in hot bathwater. No smell could be as evocative—at once she was taken back to her childhood when, at holiday time, she came to stay at Greenways with Auntie May.

There were long, joyous days spent in the heat of the fields and the garden, followed by a good farmhouse tea of fresh eggs and home-cured ham. And then the nightly bath.

'My, but you're as grubby as a piglet! Use some of that nice smelly soap I got for my birthday.' Auntie May's light, happy voice echoed around Anna's head and the seconds slipped heedlessly past as she remembered.

Then the bathroom door creaked open and suddenly, with the flow of warm air, she realised she was wasting time. As she turned towards the spare room at the end of the passage, she nearly collided with Ros, now pink-faced and fresh, although still dressed in her shabby skirt and top.

'Oh, I'm sorry—here, let me help.'

32

'It's all right. I can manage.' But Anna let the girl take the pillows from her.

In the small room they made up the bed together silently, consciously avoiding one another's eyes. Eventually Ros said, in a small voice, 'I won't be a nuisance, I promise. I'll keep out of your way and—'

As she paused, Anna looked up sharply, to see momentary apprehension flitting over her face, replaced at once by the more customary determination. Ros went on, '... And when I've had the baby, I'll go away. I'll—I'll probably have it adopted.'

She met Anna's startled gaze, then let her eyes drop at once. 'I mean, it'd be better really, wouldn't it? I could get a job then. They say if you let a baby go at once you don't have time to get fond of it—so—so that's what I'll do.'

Anna watched the girl's tense fingers playing with still-damp tendrils of hair. 'Adopted?' she asked slowly. 'Well, I suppose you could—but...'

Ros stared, suddenly hard-faced and distant. 'It's my baby, I can do what I like. I don't care what you think.'

'Why should you? As you say, it's certainly nothing to do with me.' At the door she glanced coldly over her shoulder, eyeing the battered canvas bag which Ros had brought with her. 'I'll get the meal ready. You can put your bits and pieces away later. There's a brush and comb on the dressing-table—come down

33

when you're ready.'

Pete was already in the kitchen, his face concerned, but his manner as deliberate and calm as ever. Anna knew he wouldn't talk about the girl unless she did. Almost savagely, she said. 'Well, she's here, and I hope you're pleased. I'm certainly not, but that's my affair, I suppose. Got round you, didn't she, with her sweet talk and pretty smile...'

She clattered the oven door as she removed the chicken casserole she'd been cooking, and avoided Pete's stare as she put the plates on the table.

'Maybe she did,' he agreed mildly. 'But she reminded me of a cat having kittens in the open. And I thought that you're always so kind to animals that you'd be bound to feel like that about her, too. I'm sorry if I forced you into doing something against your will, Mrs Hoskins.'

Ros's step sounded in the doorway. Anna threw Pete an exasperated glance, and went on serving the chicken. 'Come and sit down, then,' she said brusquely. 'I expect you're hungry. When did you last eat?'

Ros hesitated, before sinking heavily into the chair beside Pete. She crumbled the bread on her side plate. 'Yesterday.'

'What?' Anna turned to look at her and for the first time saw Ros's insecurity and loneliness staring back at her. Just for a moment, she was every misunderstood teenage

34

girl who has made a mistake and been cast out by her family.

Anna's heart suddenly swelled. She put a large helping of chicken and vegetables on Ros's plate and said quietly. 'Eat it up. You're going to need all your strength very soon, my girl.'

After the meal was cleared away Pete went outside to mend a broken catch on the bonnet of the van, returning just as Anna carried a tray of coffee into the sitting-room. She smiled gratefully at him. 'Thanks, Pete. Here's your reward—' He accepted a mug and went to sit beside Ros on the little two-seater couch.

The quiet serenity of the old house seemed to enclose them as they sat together, silent and thoughtful, sipping their coffee. After a little while, Anna felt relaxed enough to ask some questions. 'Won't your mother be anxious about you, Rosalind?'

The girl's face fell. 'No,' she answered shortly. 'Just as long as I'm not fouling up her reputation she'll have no worries.'

'But'—despite disliking Gilly Leach, as she did, Anna still felt a grudging sense of responsibility towards her—'you ought to let her know that you're safe,' she said firmly.

To her surprise, Pete chimed in. He smiled down at the tense girl beside him.

'I'll do it for you, if you like. Give her a ring—just say you're OK and with friends—something like that, shall I?'

35

Ros's lips trembled uncertainly and she put down the mug of coffee before answering. 'I don't know why you should care about her feelings. She certainly didn't bother about mine.'

'I've got a lively imagination,' he said drily, but his smile robbed the words of any humour and Ros looked at him.

'Well—she won't be asking the police to find me, or anything like that, but perhaps she might just be a bit worried.' She stared hard at Pete, her smile fading. 'But why should you care? She's not your mother.'

Pete held her gaze. 'I never had one. She dumped me in a home when I was too young to remember her. I just thought that if I did have a mum—well, I wouldn't treat her like you're treating yours.'

His quiet, almost casual voice seemed to echo around the room and Anna saw Ros flush. Her own feelings were certainly not comfortable; she wasn't used to this sort of frank conversation. She and Ray had never brought their emotions into the open.

Now, with surprise, she knew she agreed with Pete. Suddenly, she heard herself saying, 'The phone's in the hall. You needn't say where you are, but you could just set her mind at rest.'

Ros stared uncertainly at both of them. Then she rose, disappeared into the hall, and closed the door behind her.

Pete put his empty mug neatly on the tray

36

and stood up. 'Thanks, Mrs Hoskins. I'll be off now. Want to get on with my redecorating. Good night.' His broad smile held its usual sunny warmth, and Anna felt a loss as he went out. She heard the back door shut and knew she was alone now with Ray's daughter. Knew, too, that this was an ideal time for some plain talking.

When Ros returned, she seemed more relaxed, and sat down with a shy smile in Anna's direction. Anna waited. It wouldn't do to press too hard, although she was curious to know what Gilly Leach had said.

Suddenly Ros's voice broke into her thoughts. 'She was worried; she cried when she knew it was me.'

Carefully, Anna said, 'I'm glad you rang.'

'Yes, so am I. She's not really so bad, but she's terribly conventional. Never wanted me to go to London and try to get into modelling. If she'd had her way, I'd still be in pigtails and school uniform!' The fragile, pale face lit up a little.

Encouraged, Anna asked, 'When did you leave home, Rosalind?'

'A couple of years ago—just after my seventeenth birthday. Mum was always going on about getting a secure job and settling down, but I knew I had to do what I wanted. I liked London, there was so much happening there. And I found a job—of sorts.' Ros looked at Anna beneath thick, curling lashes, and a mischievous grin touched her face briefly. 'Mum wouldn't have liked it at all! I worked as a waitress in a downtown café...'

'At least it was work. Better than being on the dole.'

Ros nodded. 'But not what she wanted for me. You don't know her ... she's had a hard time, and now all she wants is security and for everyone to think well of her.' She hesitated.

'Her husband—he was called Dan, I didn't know him—died very suddenly over twenty years ago. She said he was an engineer, travelling all around the world on contract work. He sounds very tough, a bit of a bully, too. She was no good at coping with things and so, when he came home, he organised it all for her.

'You know, insurance, bank accounts, all the things that women aren't supposed to be able to understand!' Again, that grin came, fading as suddenly as it flashed out. 'So I suppose, when he died, and she met your Ray, well, she was swept off her feet, as they say. He was so kind, she said.'

Anna's throat was very dry. She swallowed uncomfortably. 'Did she—your mother—tell you any more about him? About—them?'

Ros sighed, kicked off her sandals and tucked bare legs under her, settling down cosily in the corner of the couch. 'A bit here and there. Sounded like the real thing to me, but of course, it couldn't last. I mean, he was

38

reluctant to divorce you.'

The casual word bit deep into Anna's returning self-control. She waited for a long moment until her heart stopped racing. Divorce? She and Ray? But there had never been any question of such an awful thing! The girl was wrong; she was making it all up.

Angrily, Anna leaned forward and stared into Ros's face. 'I don't believe you! It wasn't like that. Ray and I were happy, I tell you.'

Ros raised a cool eyebrow. 'Have it your own way. There's none so blind as those who don't want to see, or so I'm told.'

'But...' Anna sat back, trembling. She locked her hands together, and tried to ignore the menacing uncertainty that threatened.

Suddenly Ros was by her side. 'Look, Mrs Hoskins, I don't want to add to your unhappiness. But you asked me about them, and so I told you. Maybe some of it's not quite true, I don't know. Remember that my mum was deeply unhappy, too. And when people are miserable they often tell themselves lies to make themselves feel better.'

Anna forced herself to meet the direct gaze. 'Yes', she admitted slowly. 'I know that. We all do it, I suppose. Yes, well...'

They looked at one another until Ros ventured a hesitant smile. 'I'd like to go to bed, if you don't mind. It's been a long day.'

The spell was broken. Anna took a deep breath and made herself step back into the

39

safety of everyday happenings. 'That's a good idea, Rosalind. Tomorrow I'll drive you down to the Health Centre in the village and you can fix things up with my doctor. He's a nice man—youngish. And he cares. You'll be all right with him.'

At the door, Ros hid a yawn as she glanced back. 'Great. I'll feel better when I know I've got somewhere organised. The baby's due in two days, you see.'

'So soon...' Anna's uneasiness fled, and she looked at the girl with a smile.

'I'll be OK. Thanks to you.' Ros hesitated a moment longer and her face lit up with shy warmth. 'Good night. And—could you call me Ros? Mum always insisted on Rosalind, and it's such a mouthful. I'd like it if you said Ros ... if you don't mind.'

'I'd like it, too. Good night, then, Ros.'

Alone, Anna sat for a long time thinking about all Ros had told her. Try as she might, it was hard now to continue seeing Gilly Leach as a scarlet woman; she sounded a poor thing, and maybe Ray had been right to try to help her.

Anna closed her eyes as uncharacteristic emotions swept through her. Yes, she could admit it now—Ray had been a kind, gentle, and thoughtful man. So why had she always pushed him into a compartment labelled idle and soft?

She bowed her head, and, for perhaps the

40

first time in her adult life, knew the distress of guilt and shame. She and Ray could have been so much more to one another if only she hadn't insisted on going her own way.

But all she'd thought of had been the farm, the business, the land. Those had been her gods for the last twenty years, and abruptly she realised they were false. If only she had worked as hard on love and companionship.

At last she rose wearily, her body stiff, and her brain emotionally exhausted. She would sleep tonight, she knew. Passing the spare bedroom, she paused, and surprisingly felt herself relax. It was quite nice to know there was someone else in the house.

She got ready for bed with a strange feeling that fate had touched her today; she stood at a crossroad, and must decide which course to follow. Life couldn't stand still, casting backward, unhappy shadows. For good or ill, it was moving forward, and she must move with it.

*   *   *

Freddie's quiet rap on the back door came as Anna and Ros were clearing the breakfast table. As he entered, Anna gave him a brief smile, half-glad to see him, yet wishing at the same time that he'd kept out of the way for another few days. How would he take meeting Ray's illegitimate daughter? Perhaps it would

41

be best not to tell him.

Off-handedly, she nodded towards Ros. 'The daughter of a friend of mine. She's come to stay for a bit. Ros, this is my neighbour and good friend, Freddie Freeman.'

While putting away dishes, she listened to his greetings.

'Hello, there—my word, don't I know you? Haven't we met before somewhere?'

Ros met the query with a good-natured smile, and a cool reply. 'You'll have to do better than that, Mr Freeman; that sort of pick-up's old hat!'

Freddie flushed, but stood his ground. 'I wasn't being offensive, young lady—just meant what I said. I know I've seen you—or someone like you.'

'It's unlikely.' Ros came to Anna's side, leaning against the big dresser. She looked back over her shoulder at Freddie, glanced at Anna, and then said, 'I'm Ray's daughter. You might as well know—he had an affair with my mum.'

Oh, the outspokenness of youth, Anna thought, suddenly feeling quick anger. How dare she tell the whole world like that? Now there would have to be explanations and excuses, more soul-bearing, and...

Freddie's calm voice cut through her anguish. 'Ah! So you're the long-kept secret, are you? Well, hello, my dear—I knew your father well. You look very like him—and that's

42

a compliment!'

Anna whirled around, aghast. 'You knew?' she cried. 'All the time? A long-kept secret, you said . . . did he tell you, then? Oh, Freddie—and you've never said a—'

'I couldn't hurt you, old girl.' Freddie's face fell momentarily.

Anna was silenced for once, unable to snap back at him. A doormat, she'd always privately thought him, for ever under her feet; but now that image, too, was fading fast. Was nothing as it seemed?

Freddie had kept all this a secret. Freddie had an unimagined strength of mind and character. She felt suddenly that she didn't really know him at all.

He met her questioning gaze with a directness that stunned her. 'Everyone knew about Ray and Gilly, love. I just made sure that you didn't get to hear. And when it was over, he asked me not to let on. So I didn't. But now—well, you know at last, don't you?'

Anna was unable to speak for a moment as her mind whirled.

While she had been planting, hoeing, and harvesting year after year, the outside world had been plotting and observing and commenting all around her.

Why hadn't she sensed what was going on? Surely she couldn't have been all that blind and deaf?

CHAPTER THREE

Now Anna saw reassurance on Freddie's kind face, and numbly whispered the truth, as it seared through her. 'I was too busy with the farm. Ray didn't really matter. No one did. Only me—and Greenways.'

'You worked damn hard, old girl.'

He was making excuses; so he didn't condemn her ...

Angrily, Anna said, 'Too damn hard! I should have known that Ray wasn't happy.'

Ros's voice broke in, edgy and impatient. 'Look, I don't want to hear all this. It's nothing to do with me, your past life. I just want to get organised about the baby. Can we go and see the doctor, like you said? After all, tomorrow is the day ...'

Anna met the young, accusing eyes and knew she was right. Stiffly, she took off her apron and hung it up, then found the car keys.

'I'm ready,' she said flatly. 'It only takes nine or ten minutes to get there. No need to worry. You'd better take your things, in case he decides to put you in hospital right away.'

Ros went upstairs, and Anna looked around for Freddie. He was there, right behind her, a source of strength she had never appreciated before. Now it struck her forcibly that maybe there were other facets of life and friendship and love which she had also ignored in the past.

As she returned his solemn smile, she badly wanted to say something of the kind for, for the first time in years, she was seeing things more clearly, feeling deeper emotions.

'Freddie,' she said warmly, 'I wish—' and then stopped as Ros came into the room and suddenly gave a cry, reaching for the nearest chair. 'What is it?' Anna asked, immediately anxious.

'The pains. They're making me feel quite sick.' Ros glanced up in pale-faced wonder. 'Do you think it's time?'

'Yes, I do. Come on, Ros, let's get you into the van. Freddie, will you lock up after me? I'll let you know what happens.'

As she switched on the ignition, he appeared at the van window. 'I'll look after things here, Anna.' He turned to Ros. 'Good luck, my dear.' Ros, now slumped in the passenger seat, was trembling, fingers clasping her stomach. 'You'll be all right. You're in good hands with Anna. She'll see you through,' Freddie assured her.

The van roared away and Anna saw, in the mirror, how he stood, waving, until they left the house behind. She drove in silence for a few minutes, then heard Ros say almost to herself. 'He's a good friend. You're lucky to have someone like that.'

Long after Ros had disappeared into the little cottage hospital, Anna sat in the parked van outside, thinking, remembering how the girl had been taken away looking distraught and frightened, her sweating fingers lingering in Anna's firm hand as she whispered, 'You'll come and see me, won't you? Don't leave me alone—'

Words and faces jostled in her mind and, for once, she didn't care about the duties that waited back at Greenways Farm. Incidents newly experienced were far more important; Freddie, suddenly so strong and helpful, Ros, afraid and pleading—the idea of friendship, in itself a new concept in her, until now, so self-centred life.

Ray had always had friends and she'd teased him about needing other people, even while congratulating herself on her own self-sufficiency. Vaguely, she wondered what his friends had thought of her when they talked about his affair with Gilly Leach. Had they felt sorry for her? Or, perhaps they felt she deserved all she got.

A terrible bitterness swept over her and, in near-panic, she switched on the engine and drove back to the smallholding and the work that waited for her. She could no longer think straight and all she wanted was to surrender herself, once again, to the demands of the garden and the fields.

Yes, she knew she was a coward; but for the moment she'd had more than she could take. She couldn't bear to think of the baby that was now on its way. Ray's grandchild. And nothing at all to do with her.

A telephone call early next morning brought the news that Ros had a baby son. 'A lovely, healthy boy, and his mum's fine, too,' the sister said warmly. 'You can come and see them any time, no need to wait for visiting hours.' She hung up and Anna slowly replaced the receiver.

Thank goodness everything was all right. She was greatly relieved. But to go and see them? Now? It wasn't at all what she'd expected. Maybe in a few day's time, dressed neatly and with her feelings under lock and key, taking grapes and a couple of women's magazines, yes. But—straight away? In her working jeans and crumpled shirt? And she had nothing to take.

In her mind, she heard Ros's last, pleading words; 'Don't leave me alone.' Immediately, she went upstairs, hurriedly changing her shirt, running a comb through her short hair, knowing instinctively that Ros wouldn't care what she wore. What the girl needed was a human being who cared about her. All right then, she was ready...

*   *   *

The small, country hospital was abuzz with activity and voices when Anna walked into reception and was directed to the maternity wing. At the door of the long, airy ward that

47

looked out over fertile fields, touched with the morning sun, she stopped.

What should she say? How should she react? It wasn't as if Ros meant anything to her—the girl was Ray's child, not hers. She hung back, wishing she hadn't come.

A nurse bustled in behind her. 'Looking for the new mum, are you? You grannies are all the same, can't wait to start spoiling your grandchildren! Ros is over there, by the window...'

Anna recoiled, longing to shout that she wasn't a grannie and never would be, but then she looked across the ward and saw Ros watching her.

The girl's face was weary, her expression a mixture of the usual defiance and need. But Ray's eyes smiled out, and Anna suddenly knew what she must do.

Quick steps took her to the bedside and she put her arms around the girl, kissing the pale cheeks with surprising vitality. 'Congratulations! I'm so pleased for you, Ros—'

As she leaned back and found a chair, Anna watched Ros's reaction closely. She had surprised herself with the emotion she'd felt just then, but as Ros very gradually relaxed, and gave a brief, unsure smile, she knew intuitively that this was an important time in her life. The birth of Ray's grandchild.

'Let me see him, then—the baby. Have you

decided on a name?'

Tenderly, Ros drew down the shawl around the tiny head in the cot lying close to the bed. She gave Anna a proud look. 'Here he is. Thomas Ray Leach. Just on seven pounds. And look at his hair!'

Young Thomas Ray certainly had a fine head of downy black hair. He awoke, clenching miniature fists and puckering his red, baby face for a moment. Then, suddenly he was asleep again, as peaceful as an angel. As beautiful, too.

Anna's stomach knotted tightly. Harry had been like this. Her little Harry ... But she wouldn't spoil Ros's joy. She blinked hard, sat back on her chair, smiled and looked around the ward while Ros chatted happily.

All the nurses had been wonderful. She'd wanted a boy. Wasn't it marvellous that it was all over?

Listening, Anna smiled and said yes and no at the right times, but her thoughts were elsewhere.

She was shockingly aware that there were no loving cards or flowers crowding the bare table at Ros's bedside. No visitors, save herself, to sit and admire, pouring out their love on the new mother, helping her to adjust to this, the greatest step in a woman's life.

Ros was completely alone. Except for her—

When Ros hesitantly began to say that she had a favour to ask, Anna nodded at once.

49

'Anything I can do,' she said quietly.

'It's Keith, my boy-friend.' Ros gestured towards the cot. 'Tom's father. He ought to know—don't you think?' Her eyes questioned Anna anxiously. 'Oh, I know we split up, but, well, I'd like him to know he has a son.' Ros flushed. 'I don't want any more secrets.'

Anna hid the deep sigh that arose within her. Ros was right, of course. Secrets only led to pain and distress.

'Very well,' she said resignedly. 'I'll bring you some paper and you can drop him a note.'

'No—I'd like you to phone him. It's only London, it won't cost much. Just tell him about Tom. And say I'm OK. That's all.' Ros looked at her beseechingly.

Anna didn't relish the idea of speaking to the uncaring young lout who had got the girl into trouble and then not bothered with her. But, if that was what Ros wanted...

'I'll ring him when I get home. And I'll come and see you again tonight.' With flowers and cards from herself and Pete and Freddie; with as much friendship as she could find inside herself to give.

Ros's smile was thanks enough. As Anna rose to leave, the girl pushed a grubby slip of paper into her hand at the last moment, with a Hounslow telephone number scrawled on it.

'His name's Keith Turner. Thanks, Mrs Hoskins—I'm really grateful.'

Anna drove back to Greenway Farm in a

mood of strange enchantment. The sky was an unclouded blue, and June flowers glimmered and shone beneath the benevolent sun. The world was bright and beautiful. Somehow, she felt close to Ray—wherever he was.

But when she rang the number Ros had given her, she was greeted by a casual London voice saying no, Keith wasn't there. Could she leave a message, they would see him later. A son! That was great! Keith would be really pleased to hear that one.

Anna went into the garden feeling angry, for no real reason. It took her a good hour's weeding to discover why she'd had such an abrupt change of mood. She was surprised at the instant dislike she'd taken to Keith Turner, whoever he might be. He didn't deserve to have a baby son.

She paused, fingers deep in rich warm soil, and added indignantly to herself that he didn't deserve a nice girl like Ros, either—so brave and so determined to get by on her own.

And then she remembered something. Ros had said she would have the baby adopted. Thomas Ray—given to some other woman to love and bring up? Anna stumbled back to the kitchen to prepare bread and cheese for lunch, and felt all the joy had gone from the day.

But when she stood at Ros's bedside again that evening, arms full of flowers, and fondly-worded cards, there were more surprises still to come.

51

Ros's face was happy, but anxious. 'What do you think?' she said lightly. 'Keith phoned! He got your message, put two and two together, and found me here. We had quite a chat.'

Anna sat down heavily. 'That's nice,' she said without much feeling.

'Yes. He's coming down to see me. I mean us.' Ros's hand lingered over the downy black head. There was a new ring to her voice, an unfamiliar sparkle in the sea-green eyes.

She looked at Anna over the top of the bunch of sweet-smelling cottage pinks that she still held, and added bravely, yet with an underlying note of the old defiance, 'You know what I said about adoption? Well, I've decided not to . . .'

Anna's heart raced, and she felt her face light up as Ros added, very quietly, very humbly. 'I couldn't lose him now. He means the world to me.'

For a long moment their eyes met, and held. 'Do you think I'm being silly, Mrs Hoskins—to keep him I mean?'

Anna looked at Thomas Ray, small and pink and perfect, and answered in the same, quiet way, 'No, Ros. I'm sure you're doing the right thing. And if you need any help—well, I'll be here . . .'

But, driving away from the hospital, reality asserted itself once more and Anna faced the future with misgivings. Ros had a child to bring up, by herself. That was hard enough, but this Keith person was coming down to see her, and that could only complicate matters.

Turning into the gateway of the farm, Anna knew a strange feeling of determination, quite different from anything she had previously experienced. It was something she was feeling for someone else, no longer for herself; already she knew she felt fondness and compassion for Ros and the baby, it wouldn't take much more for it to turn into love.

They could stay at Greenways, with her— and Keith Turner wouldn't be allowed to have anything to do with either of them.

*   *   *

It was late the next afternoon when Anna answered a loud bang at the door and found a handsome young man, tow-haired and dressed in a clean, neat suit, on the step.

He seemed very sure of himself, she thought. 'Hi! I'm Keith Turner. You must be Mrs Hoskins—right?'

She stared, taking in his unexpectedly conventional appearance. 'Yes, I am.' Truth to tell, she hadn't been prepared for such easy charm and attraction. But her determination held firm; she refused to like him. 'Have you been to see Ros?' she asked coldly.

'You bet I have—and the baby. He's a little smasher, isn't he? Looks like me, don't you think?'

Anna smiled cautiously. Such enthusiasm was dangerously infectious.

'He's certainly a lovely child.' She loosened up a little. 'Come in, then. Would you like a cup of tea?'

'Thanks. Ros said you were a good friend. She sent her love, by the way.'

'That's nice.' Anna felt a glow inside her. After putting on the kettle, she turned towards the boy, now sitting in Ray's old chair by the stone fireplace. 'So you've come down from London?' She wasn't usually a chatty woman, but the fresh, keen face looking all about the kitchen seemed to warrant some friendly conversation.

Keith shot her a big grin. 'Yeah. Left the old smoke behind for a while. Mrs Hoskins—can I ask a favour?'

Surprised, Anna blinked at the brilliant hazel eyes, suddenly wary of the confident smile so impetuously directed at her. 'What is it?'

'Ros wondered if you'd let me use her bed for the night. I can't get a decent train back at this time of day—better if I stayed till tomorrow, then I could see her again before I go. Is that all right with you?'

'Well, I suppose...' He was up and by her side, all smiles and gratitude before she could find a reasonable excuse to say no.

'You're really nice, you know, just like Ros said! Thanks, Mrs Hoskins.'

And so it was decided. Anna smiled without meaning to. Obviously Keith Turner was a young man of great persuasion and used to getting his own way. She began to understand how Ros must feel about him—loving him one moment, regretting his influence on her life the next.

'All right, then. Just for tonight,' she conceded, pouring boiling water into the brown teapot and then handing him a cup. They sat down in silence until, suddenly the barriers broke and the conversation began.

'Super place you've got—' Keith grinned, in the same devastating way he had earlier. 'Ros was telling me how much she liked it here.'

Anna swallowed, taken aback at such affability when she had fully expected him to be a layabout without manners or feelings. 'Does Ros know yet when she's coming home?' She was a bit wary about the word home but it came to her so naturally, making her feel quite astounded. She hadn't realised that Ros had so soon become part of her life.

'Tomorrow, that dragon of a sister said. Nearly bit my head off, she did.'

Anna could well imagine the situation, with Sister Moran being unwillingly charmed out of her usual dictatorial efficiency. Hiding a smile, she said quietly, 'Ros is in good hands there.'

He relaxed, sitting back in the shabby old cane chair and looking quite at ease.

Anna felt curiosity stir. 'All I know about

you is your name,' she said, a little defiantly. 'Ros didn't tell me much more—'

'No, she wouldn't. Ros is a great girl but— well, we had our ups and downs She went off before I could stop her after we had a row, and then it seemed a good idea to split for a while. But now—well, we might just make it up again. We'll just have to wait and see, eh?'

Very carefully, Anna said, 'You mean, live together again? In London? Maybe Ros will join you there?' Something shrank inside her. This wasn't at all what she had anticipated.

'Not necessarily in London. I can live where I like—I've no real ties at the moment.' Keith laughed, showing white, even teeth.

'No, I daresay not.' Anna eyed him sharply. 'What do you do for a living then?'

For a second the smile died, and a quick frown narrowed his bright, knowledgeable eyes. Then the charm was back, smooth as ever. 'I don't really have a steady job at the moment. But I work at this and that—make a penny or two wherever it crops up. You know the sort of thing...'

Oh, yes. Indeed she did. So, he lived from day to day. Suddenly Anna knew why Ros had left him, charming as he seemed. Unreliable and feckless, selfish, an opportunist, only thinking of himself. And yet, so immensely likeable...

Against her will, she smiled wryly. 'And now you're a father, will you settle down? Change

56

your way of life?'

The bright, flecked eyes met hers without a shadow of guilt. 'I might even do that, Mrs Hoskins. If Ros and I can find somewhere we'd both like to stay.' The smile was open and endearing, but Anna sensed a hint of something she didn't like in the last words. Briskly, she got up and began to prepare the evening meal.

'Pete and I usually eat about six. Maybe you'd like to join us?'

'No, thanks. I'll have a wander round the village, get a snack in the pub, maybe. Then I'll go and see Ros again. I'll be back—what, about ten o'clock?'

'Don't make it later. I go to bed early and—' She stopped abruptly, not wanting to add her thoughts: and I don't intend to leave a key with you. She knew, instinctively, that he was the sort who would wander about the house, prying here, probing there, seeing what he could find, and assessing how much everything was worth.

Then she relented. He was a bit pushy, that was all. A typical young man of the times. Harry might have been like this, had he lived.

'Come upstairs and I'll show you the bedroom.' She smiled over her shoulder as they went into the hall together.

'Thanks, Mrs Hoskins.' He smiled. 'This is really nice of you.'

Pete came into the kitchen as Anna was dishing up the meal and Keith was about to leave. She introduced them and watched their reactions; they seemed to be sizing each other up—both wary and slightly aggressive.

Keith nodded casually across the room. 'Hi! Finished for the day, then? Cushy job you country types have.' The wry grin was friendly, but Pete stiffened immediately.

'Dunno 'bout that. Gardening's hard work. Not like sitting about in offices or shops.'

'Yeah?' A note of scorn gave an edge to Keith's London accent. 'What d'you know about city life, mate? You got it made down here—roses round the door, and your tea all ready for you. I don't suppose you know a teapot from a saucepan, do you? Now me, I'm a good cook. Got to be, living like I do.'

Pete's face took on his well-known vacant look and Anna flinched. When he was being got at he became obstinate, seeming suddenly to act far dumber than he was. She did hope that this initial sparring didn't mean real enmity to come...

Pete's stolid voice cut through her fears. 'Maybe you're right. But I enjoy it nevertheless.'

They stared at each other in hostile silence. Then Anna gave Keith a playful shove and the tension broke. 'Get along with you,' she said.

'You'll be late at the hospital.'

'See you, then,' Keith said shortly, turning to the door.

'Yes,' Pete replied. 'Shouldn't be surprised if you do.'

While dishing up the meal, Anna watched Pete go to the window, following Keith's figure down the path and out of sight. Then he disappeared to clean up. When he returned to the kitchen he sat down and said, almost savagely, 'How long's he here for, Mrs Hoskins? That Turner chap?'

'Just tonight. He's catching an early train back to London tomorrow.'

'Ros is too darn good for him!' Pete dug into his tea moodily, and quick irritation rose inside Anna. Men, she thought, always so aggressive, always ready for a fight.

'How do you know?' she countered coolly. 'You've only just met him and already you're putting him down. He's not so bad, not really.'

Pete gave her a long, thoughtful stare. 'Well, I don't like him,' he said firmly, returning to his meal.

'That's a pity.' For some reason she found herself backing Keith up.

As she pushed the vegetable dish across the table, Pete asked, 'Where will he sleep next time?'

Anna thought hard before answering, avoiding Pete's baleful stare as she did so. 'I'm sure Freddie'll give him a bed.' She smiled gently. 'After all, if they decide to marry they'll need some time to discuss their plans.'

'Marry!' Pete's eyebrows shot up and the words growled out. 'She's not going to marry that—that yob, is she?'

'Why not? He's the father of her child.' Anna heard the bitterness in her words and felt anger rise.

'Look,' she said fiercely, 'Keith Turner is here because I've said he can stay. It's none of your business, Pete. So don't start making trouble, please.'

Pete looked wounded. He ate silently and didn't reply, but the look on his face was enough to let Anna know that she had spoken too sharply. Remorse made her try to make amends.

'I'm sorry, Pete. But I've got enough on my plate without you and Keith being at loggerheads.'

'That's all right, Mrs Hoskins. I understand.'

Oh, what a muddle she was making of things. She got to her feet and went out of the room, banging the door loudly and wishing life wasn't so terribly complicated.

Just as she had foreseen, Keith persuaded her to let him stay for the week-end, so that he and Ros could talk and make some plans. In the morning Anna phoned Freddie, asking for the use of his spare room, and was amazed when, instead of the expected quick consent, was told quite firmly that he didn't want to have the chap in his house.

'But you've never met him! He only arrived last night—' Anna's voice rose in protest.

'Oh, yes, I have, old girl. He came sniffing round here before he got to you. Asked me where you lived, and so on. And had a good look at my pictures. I didn't ask him in, but there he was, in the hall before you could say Jack Robinson. Crafty sort of bloke, I thought.'

'That's not fair, Freddie.' Anna bristled, even though he was only voicing her own thoughts. 'You only met him once...'

'And that was enough. Look, love, I know the sort of fellow he is. I've lived up there, see. Wide boys—'

Anna broke in firmly. 'He may not be the sort to trust with the family silver, but I should be grateful if you'd take him for a couple of nights, Freddie. I've—well, I've promised. And I've only got the one spare bed, and, and...'

'Say no more, love. You've landed yourself in it, I can see. Sure he can come. But he'd better watch those sticky fingers. No one's going to make off with any of my treasures!'

'Of course not, Freddie! He's not a thief, for heaven's sake.'

Freddie sounded unnaturally grim. 'Let's hope not.' Then his voice softened. 'All right, Anna. Any chance of seeing you soon?'

'Of course.' Having won a victory, Anna felt

61

compelled to invite him to supper. 'Come tonight. Ros is bringing the baby home this afternoon, we'll have a celebration party.'

'We?'

'All of us. Ros, Keith, you, me—Pete—' Uneasiness stabbed inside her. She hoped there would be no aggression between the two boys. Or with Freddie, who already seemed very prejudiced. 'Freddie,' she added hesitantly, 'I don't want any trouble. Keith and Pete are young, and—'

He laughed quietly. 'And Rosalind is a smasher. I take your meaning, love. Don't worry, I'll act as peacemaker. I'll bring a bottle of wine, shall I? That should cement good relations.'

*   *   *

It seemed at first that her fears were ill-founded. Keith brought Ros and Tom home in a taxi and didn't hesitate when Anna told him he was to sleep at Freddie's bungalow, down the road.

'Fine,' Keith said airily. 'It'll give me a chance to look at some more of his work. Curious old boy, all art and no business head, I'd say. Does he ever sell anything?'

Anna stiffened. 'I can't say. That's his affair, not mine.' Nor yours, she might have added, but Ros was listening, her gentle face strained and vulnerable.

Anna berated herself. 'My dear, come and sit down. What am I thinking of, keeping you standing here? Let's put young Tom upstairs for a while, and you can rest as well. I got Pete to take a nice comfy chair into your room this morning...'

'I don't need to rest, Mrs Hoskins. I'm right as rain—the hospital said so. But I'm glad to be back again. It was OK there, but ... well, it's not like home, is it?'

At the top of the stairs, Anna paused, looking back, as Ros nearly collided with her. 'Home,' she echoed blankly, meeting the suddenly uncertain eyes. That word again. 'Do you think of Greenways as your home now, Ros?' she asked bluntly, and watched the pale face set in mutinous, wounded lines.

But Ros had no chance to reply, for Keith, following at her heels, clinched the matter. Putting his arm around her, he smiled blandly into Anna's face. 'Home is where the heart is—wouldn't you say so, Mrs Hoskins? And we can make a home wherever we are.' He turned to Ros, dropping a kiss on her upturned face. 'Now, don't go making Mrs Hoskins feel she's got to offer to let us stay here, Ros, love.'

Anna caught her breath. Oh, the cunning insolence of it! What a young opportunist he was. But, even as she smouldered with annoyance, the meaning of his remark made her smile.

Leading the way into Ros's room, she

63

managed to say quite calmly, 'That's something we'll have to talk about later. Let's get the week-end over with first.'

Unwillingly, she left them alone, with Tom, bundled in his shawl, asleep on the middle of the bed, and Keith, his arms still around Ros, standing by the window with her, looking down at the garden and the vegetable field for all the world as if he owned the smallholding himself.

In the kitchen she snapped at Pete when he came in for dinner. 'You're too early, I haven't had time yet—what with Ros coming back, and Keith—' She saw the expression on his pleasant face grow hard and unyielding, and told herself she must manage the situation better than this.

Sighing, she smiled at him apologetically. 'Sorry, sorry! I'm just not used to having so many people around the house. I'll get the dinner ready now—give me a couple of minutes, Pete.'

He nodded silently, and went off to the downstairs cloakroom to wash. By the time she'd put fresh bread and cheese on the table and whipped up a quick salad, he was back, sitting quietly, reading the paper.

'I see the Flower Show Committee is getting under way. Putting anything in this year, Mrs Hoskins?'

They were deep in a horticultural discussion when footsteps sounded, and Ros and Keith

64

came in, looking a little shy, but with a glow on her face that stabbed deep at Anna's emotions.

'Are we late? Sorry, we were talking.' Ros sat down, making sure that Keith took the chair next to her. The meal proceeded in uneasy silence, which Anna tried to break by asking Keith what he was working on at the moment.

'Not much really.' He helped himself to a huge spoonful of green tomato chutney. 'My business travels with me, actually.' He slid her a crafty look. 'I'm always on the look-out for contacts. Houses selling up. Auctions. Things that people don't want which will fetch a useful penny.'

Pete rattled the paper under his nose. 'There's a jumble sale in the village hall this afternoon,' he said without any expression in his voice. 'You'll get there for the opening, if you hurry.'

He glanced at the clock on the wall. 'Two o'clock sharp, and twenty pence to get in. Want to borrow my wheelbarrow for all your bargains?'

Anna held her breath, staring at Keith, who had stopped in the middle of a large mouthful to scowl at Pete. The good-looking face turned an ugly red, and the jawline set tensely as the muscles twitched in anger.

For a second no one spoke, and Anna felt the air thicken with hostility. She saw Ros look uneasily first at Keith and then at Pete, who went on with his meal as if nothing had

65

happened.

Then Keith put down the knife with a clatter, and dragged back his chair. 'I'll make my own arrangements about things, thanks,' he said, his voice low, and the sharp London accent more marked than usual. 'You want to watch out, my son. I've wiped out people like you, who make funny jokes at my expense...'

CHAPTER FOUR

Ros clutched at Keith's arm. 'Please don't,' she whispered nervously. 'Pete didn't mean—'

'I know what he meant all right. And he knows, too—don't you, mate? You know what I mean, eh?'

Pete looked up slowly, to meet the full impact of Keith's hard, light eyes. 'All I know, Mister Turner,' he said unconcernedly, 'is that you're out of your depth down here. We're country folk, not city slickers. And the two don't mix.' He paused, dark eyes glowing suddenly with humour, then he repeated Keith's last words in his own, slow way, 'Know what I mean, eh?'

Quickly Anna broke in. The situation was fast getting out of hand. 'Stop it, both of you. I won't have any trouble. If you want a row, have it outside, away from my house. Can't you think of Ros—just out of hospital, and

66

with a child upstairs? You ought to be ashamed of yourselves.'

By now both men looked slightly sheepish. Keith strode out of the room with Ros following. Pete pushed his empty plate away from him, glancing at Anna with thoughtful apology.

'Sorry, Mrs Hoskins. But he needled me. He's just the sort of chap I can't abide.'

'And you made it pretty obvious. Calm down, Pete—he's only here for the week-end.' But as she cleared away, Anna kept thinking of the remark she had made earlier—That's something we'll have to talk about later. Let's get the week-end over first. Now she knew, with a sense of relief at having made a decision, that the answer to any further request to stay on must be no.

It was with growing apprehension that she prepared the evening meal. But, as if to make up for earlier unpleasantness, both men behaved impeccably. Pete was his usual quiet, stolid self and, even if he did once or twice look at his adversary with something approaching dislike, he kept silent. And Keith, too, managed to exert some self-control. The evening went quite well, though, and Anna felt herself relaxing as they all moved into the sitting-room with their coffee at the end of the meal, quiet voices rising and falling in harmless topics of conversation.

She knew that Freddie had been the

mainstay of the evening, with his friendly, innocuous chatter and masterly handling of possible disagreements. Not that he'd appeared to dominate—far from it, for Ros had been persuaded to talk freely to both him and Anna, while Keith had also opened up, discussing some of his business methods. Methods, Anna recalled wryly, which might not have stood up to investigation but which had, clearly, produced financial profit.

What had he said, for instance, about selling his mother's few silver heirlooms—'I knew she was worried about the problem of insuring them. So now she has the money in the bank and no silver to clean.'

Pete yawned and stood up. 'Think I'll go to my bed. Some of us have to get up early, Sunday or not.' Just for a second, he slid a wicked glance at Keith, sprawled beside Ros on the couch with an arm around her shoulders. Before Keith could rise to the bait, Freddie said smoothly, 'Not a bad idea. I'll go, too. Coming then, Keith?'

Keith's knowing eyes slid over the watching faces, and he pulled Ros a little nearer. 'Just a minute till I say good night.' He nuzzled her hair, dismissing the rest of them as he did so.

Anna followed Pete and Freddie to the back door. Pete went off at once, but Freddie lingered. 'You'll be all right?' he asked quietly. 'Want me to hang around?'

'No, Ros will send him packing in a minute,

I'm sure. Thanks, Freddie. You've been such a help tonight.'

His warm, quick smile pierced her with its depth of affection. Then he was the old Freddie again, the doormat under her feet, the bumbling sheepdog, affectionate and undemanding.

'That's all right, old girl. Any time. Well, good night, Anna.'

She leaned forward and kissed his cheek, watching the colour flare up as he blinked, nodded rather helplessly, and then went off into the darkness.

Behind her, Keith and Ros appeared, hand in hand, Ros drawing away as Anna turned. Casually, she said, 'See you tomorrow, Keith. Good night.'

Keith stood, looking at her for a long moment. 'Good night, love. Sleep well.' His face was mocking, and he reached out to run a finger down the line of her averted face. Then he nodded casually at Anna, muttered a quick, ''Bye, then,' and followed Freddie down the path.

Alone, Anna watched Ros lift her head, her expression unfathomable. 'You're worn out, my dear,' Anna said quickly. 'Go up to bed. Young Tom will be wanting his feed. Call me if you need any help.'

Ros stood by the door, frail and pathetically thin, and it suddenly dawned on Anna that the girl badly needed caring for, not just for a week or two, but the rest of her life. She was a delicate young woman, requiring support to help her bloom in full beauty.

'Ros—' Anna's voice was uneven as she moved forward impulsively, taking Ros's hands in her own. 'Don't make up your mind about anything, not yet. It's too early. You have plenty of time. Stay here when Keith leaves—don't rush into anything. I'd like to have you—'

Ros stared and then, suddenly, tears rushed into her big, grey eyes. 'You're so kind. I wasn't sure at first what you'd be like. I thought ... But now, well—' She shrugged.

'Now I've learned a bit about myself, to tell you the truth.' Embarrassed by the show of emotion, Anna strove to be flippant. 'And I have you to thank for it, Ros. You and young Tom.'

They looked at each other with a new relationship beginning to develop. Then, out of the darkness upstairs, a tiny cry sounded. Ros smiled, her face beaming with happiness.

'There he is—spot on, as usual! I'll go up. Good night, Mrs Hoskins.' Halfway up the staircase she stopped and looked down at Anna. 'And thanks. For everything.'

*   *   *

During Sunday, Anna became aware that a new routine was imposing itself on the

70

household. No longer was the day quiet, the house empty. Ros asked to be allowed to cook lunch.

'I love cooking. And I haven't had a chance lately, not in those silly bedsits...'

The large leg of lamb that she produced, together with potatoes roasted to excellent crispness, and young, fresh vegetables from the garden, bore all the hallmarks of a natural cook, and Anna was generous with her praise. The men left nothing on the plates, and Pete commented quietly as Ros dished out the apple pie and cream, 'That was an excellent meal, Ros; you can cook for me any time.'

Anna heard, and reflected that it was just as well Keith hadn't been paying attention, and failed to notice Ros's pretty blush at the compliment and the way she returned Pete's smile.

After dinner, Anna went into the garden. Normally on a Sunday afternoon she treated herself to a quiet hour or two, but she felt it right to leave Ros and Keith alone; and it was beautiful out among her fragrant, colourful flowers.

The sun was warm on her bent back, and the satisfaction of working in the moist earth gave her a certain peace. She wondered idly about entering cut flowers for the village Flower Show later on in August; and wouldn't it be nice if Ros and Tom could come with her to meet her friends...

71

She straightened up as an idea struck her. Ros could maybe enter for the cake competition.

Before finishing her weeding, Anna paused at the end of the ancient shrubbery, where straggling bushes badly needed cutting back. Last year Pete had dumped a bag of sand there, just beneath the lilac which was now bursting out in huge purple showers.

The little pile of silver-gold grains nudged at Anna's fertile mind—a sandpit for Tom. What a perfect place, within sight and sound of the kitchen, shaded from the hot sun, and safe as houses. Yes, she could see him there already, a sturdy toddler, busy with bucket and spade.

She felt herself grow buoyant with anticipation, and then, suddenly, drop back again into the coldness of reality. Ridiculous to think that such a dream could come true. By the time Tom was old enough to play in a sandpit, he and Ros would be somewhere else, firmly established in their own lives. Even— Anna shut her eyes at the thought—even perhaps married to Keith.

The truth was stark and painful and, as she took her tools to put away in the shed, she forced herself to face her emotions, to think logically about the situation she was in.

She knew now, with an unfamiliar sense of openness, that she could easily grow to love Ros and the boy. The house would be empty when they left, her own life sadly bare. She knew now she wanted them to stay.

With Keith? Ah, that was the stumbling block. And yet, she couldn't decide quite what she felt about Keith. Good-humoured, amusing, and charming—yes, he was all of those—but the other side of him was less appealing. He was crafty, glib, aggressive, possibly even untrustworthy.

She pondered the difficult situation, and then heaved a sigh. Perhaps, after all, there would be no need for her to have to make up her mind one way or the other. Perhaps Keith would just go away and leave them alone.

During the evening, Anna listened to the chatter that floated around her. Ros astounded them halfway through the meal by producing a fresh fruit salad. 'Good for all our figures,' she'd said, with a new note of confidence and enthusiasm in her voice. Pete had looked at her keenly, while Keith raised a sardonic eyebrow.

Anna discovered she was fast becoming a watcher, an observer; she noticed how Ros seemed to be turning to Pete more than to Keith, although, of course, there was still a sense of intimacy between the girl and Keith. But when Ros smiled, the warmth was directed at Pete.

Before the evening ended, there was an uncomfortable return of the hostility which had erupted the day before, nothing too bad, but unpleasant enough to make Anna long for tomorrow when Keith would be leaving.

But, even as he departed, early on Monday morning, it seemed that he had made other plans.

He hugged Ros on the doorstep before getting into the van. Anna had thought it only right that she see him off the premises personally, and so was interrupting her usual routine of gardening to take him to the station.

Anna thought Ros looked slightly intimidated, but then Keith got in beside her and they drove off, Keith pointedly ignoring Pete's rather mocking wave from nearby.

He talked as they drove through the lush, green countryside. 'Not bad down here, is it? Might be a change to settle down among fields, for a bit. 'Course, I'll have to make contact with all my selling mates, first. I told Freddie not to expect too much too soon.'

Anna took her eyes off the road and stared, with amazement, at his self-satisfied face. 'What do you mean? What's Freddie got to do with London—or with you, come to that?'

Keith laughed. 'Didn't tell you, did I? The old boy agreed to me getting rid of some of his pictures. Money spinners, they are. 'Course, he'll have to split equally; I usually take a bigger percentage on a sale, but seeing as he's a friend of yours—'

Anna prayed for strength. 'So you really do intend to return?'

'Why not?' He seemed surprised that she might have thought otherwise. 'I'm only going

74

back to London to set myself up for moving. And I'll be down with a van to pick up Freddie's paintings soon. We could be sitting on a gold mine, Freddie and me.'

At the station he thanked her politely for her hospitality, and then delivered a last depressing blow. 'Ros and me will be fixing up something permanent, soon—once I get the money flowing in. Oh, don't worry, Mrs Hoskins, we won't be far away—I can see she means a lot to you. You'll be glad to have us around, I daresay, a woman on her own, like you.'

Anna drove back to Greenways in a state of utter confusion, feeling Keith's last words suffocating her hopes and anticipated happiness at being alone with Ros and the baby.

She halted at Freddie's bungalow. He was, as usual, painting in the garden and gave her a warm welcome. 'Nice to see you! Come in and have a coffee...' He was wreathed in smiles and she felt a burst of old irritation. Didn't he realise what was going on?

'Freddie, I can't stop long. I don't like to leave Ros alone, but—well it's about Keith. He's selling your pictures, he said.'

The smile died quickly. 'I know. Talked me into it, wouldn't listen when I said no. That young man's too free with his ideas—but I've reached a compromise with him. He can take what I don't want. Ten canvases and that's it.

75

Mind you, I daresay he'll try and get more out of me—initiative's all right, but he's got a darned sight too much!'

He looked anxiously at her set face and added, almost pleadingly, 'Nice to have a little more money, old girl. Never know when one might need a nest egg, eh?'

Anna didn't answer. She was hurt at him going along with Keith's ideas. Surely he must have seen through Keith's calculated charm? She supposed he just wasn't strong enough to say a firm no.

Wearily she turned away. 'I see. Well, I just hope he doesn't take you for a ride. He has no morals whatsoever.'

Freddie surprised her with his quiet answer. 'I don't ever condemn anyone till I know them well, Anna. It might be a good thing if you did the same.'

She stared angrily, then, refusing the coffee, flounced back to the van, not bothering to say goodbye. How dare he, she thought, not allowing herself to acknowledge the undoubted truth of his words.

Back at Greenways Farm, all was peaceful and quiet. Ros had found something loose and cool to wear, and now sat in the morning sun, while Tom slept in his carry-cot beneath the shade of the shrubbery. It was in Anna's mind to tell Ros about the sandpit, but she pushed the idea from her mind.

She'd been hurt enough already—why invite

more pain?

It was soothing, though, to notice the easy relationship that was clearly developing between Ros and Pete. And when, later that afternoon, Ros asked, slightly embarrassed, if Anna would be kind enough to listen out for Tom for an hour in the evening, because Pete had asked her to his cottage to hear a new record, she was only too pleased to help.

She put out of her mind all thoughts of Keith's return, and sat in the sitting-room, door ajar in case the baby cried, studying a new seed catalogue which had come in the day's post.

And then the telephone rang. With a deep sense of unease she went to answer it. Could it be Keith again? Already? But the voice that asked huskily, 'Is that Mrs Hoskins?' was a female one and unfamiliar. It was only when the woman said, 'This is Gilly Leach,' that Anna remembered hearing the same soft tone recently.

She sat down, grateful for support. She had forgotten Gilly Leach during the last forty-eight hours. But now she was swept once again into the remembered chasm of self-pity and resentment.

'Yes?' she said coldly. 'What do you want, Mrs Leach?'

There was a pause, then the soft voice said firmly, 'I'd like news of my grandchild, Mrs Hoskins—is that asking too much? I phoned the hospital, and they said Rosalind had had her baby, and was staying with you. That was at least two days ago. I would have thought she might have told me that I had a grandson.'

Anna took a deep, calming breath. 'You're right,' she acknowledged stiffly. 'Ros should have phoned you. But we've had such a busy week-end...' Something warned her not to mention Keith.

She waited for the soft voice to explode into paroxysms of joy at the news of the baby's safe birth, and Ros's well-being. But, instead, it said, with a new steeliness that Anna had never heard before, 'How nice for you all. And I've been sitting at home and waiting for a message that never came. But there, that's Rosalind all over. She only ever thinks of herself.'

'That's not true!' Anna couldn't help bursting out indignantly. 'Ros is a good mother, a dear girl—' She stopped abruptly, knowing she was being foolish.

Gilly Leach sighed. 'I'm glad you get on so well,' she said in the same chilly tone. 'But, of course, she's only making use of you. As soon as she finds someone else to take her in, she'll be off. I tell you, I know her. She's my daughter after all, Mrs Hoskins—'

'Yes, Mrs Leach, your daughter—and my husband's daughter, too...'

A long silence followed Anna's bitter reply. At last Gilly said, her voice a shade gentler than before, 'I think it's high time you and I

78

met, Mrs Hoskins. There are things we both need to say.

'Will you come and have tea with me? Tomorrow? Here's my address ... I'll expect you around three-thirty. Oh, and please give my love to Rosalind. I haven't forgotten her, even if she can't be bothered with her mother any more...'

The line went dead, and Anna replaced the receiver, her usually-healthy colour faded to a grey pallor. All the strain and tension of the past few weeks suddenly overcame her. She stumbled back to the sitting-room and sank down in her usual chair, staring wretchedly at the far wall.

Anna closed her eyes, wondering at the new awareness of life that Ray's death had seemingly caused.

*   *   *

Footsteps outside the back door heralded Ros's return, accompanied by Pete. Anna looked up as they entered the sitting-room, unprepared for the expression of shy happiness that relaxed Ros's usually tense face.

There was no need to ask if the record session had been enjoyable. Instead, she said quietly, 'Not a peep from upstairs. I'll make a drink while you get Tom down, shall I?'

Pete hovered in the doorway. She smiled at him as she went into the kitchen, ending his uncertainty by saying, 'Coffee or chocolate, Pete?' His answering grin stayed with her and she wondered curiously about him and Ros all the time she was preparing the tray of mugs and heating the milk.

When she returned to the sitting-room, Ros was on the couch with Tom in her arms, whispering endearments as she smoothed the dark, wispy hair from his sleepy eyes.

Anna handed Pete his drink.

They sat in companionable silence, punctuated only by Tom's small murmurs, until Pete finished his drink. He stood up, replacing the mug on the table.

'Thanks, Mrs Hoskins.' His eyes slid towards Ros. 'See you tomorrow, then?'

Ros raised her head, as she put the baby up to her shoulder and gently patted his back. 'Sure.' She smiled, and Anna, watching with discreet awareness, saw the return of the easiness which was beginning to flow between the two of them. Pete nodded, and left.

Ros's glance followed him until she met Anna's eyes, coloured very slightly, and then turned back to young Tom to busy herself with nappy-changing.

A gentle indolence filled the quiet room, and Anna leaned back in her chair, giving herself to the thoughts and memories that stirred within her.

The years started to roll back, and without any effort she found herself reliving the experience of having Harry on her knee, as a baby; he had been as fair as Tom was dark, a bundle of demanding energy, his curious eyes for ever seeking out and observing.

For the first time in many years, Anna gave in to her grief. Usually she pushed away the sadness that always lingered at the sound of Harry's name, but now it remained with her.

Silent in her chair, almost removed from the homely scene of Ros with Tom on her lap, her mind moved from one newly-realised fact to the next.

She had adored Harry, had made him the main part of her life, to the extent of excluding Ray. She bowed her head as the truth hit her. She could admit it now, relaxed and seeing things more clearly than ever before.

She didn't know that her eyes had filled with tears or that her usually self-controlled, stern face had softened with the memories; not until Ros's voice, breathless and anxious, brought her back to the present.

'Are you all right, Mrs Hoskins? You seem to be miles away. It's nothing I've done, is it?'

Anna blinked, shocked that she was so near to tears, and, after a moment's confusion, smiled reassuringly at the pale face regarding her so anxiously.

'No, no! It's not you—I was just thinking, that's all. Remembering...'

She stared down at Tom, newly changed and fed, smelling sweetly of milk and talcum

81

powder, and couldn't resist the urge to touch him. Her fingers, hard and worn, offered themselves to his groping hand, and at once he clutched her, his pink face turning to stare blindly into her adoring eyes.

For a long moment he held her fingers then, yawning, abandoned them, nuzzling into his mother and suddenly falling asleep as he did so.

Quietly, Ros said, 'He likes you. I think you'll get on well together.'

'I do hope so.'

Anna watched Ros carry the sleeping baby upstairs, returning soon after to clear up the mess of towels and tissues. By the time Ros was again settled in her usual corner of the couch, feet tucked beneath her, with a comfortably-relaxed expression on her face, Anna had made up her mind.

'I'd like to talk, Ros. Are you too tired to listen?'

Ros stirred. 'Of course not.' She raised her head attentively. 'What do you want to talk about?'

'Me,' Anna said baldly. 'Me and Ray—and Harry. Our son who died when he was only four months old. Subjects I've never discussed with anyone before. But I want to tell you now. Is that all right?'

Ros's eyes held hers for a moment. Gently, the girl smiled then nodded. 'Go on. I'm listening.'

It all came rushing out, now that the dam of silence had been breached, and Anna felt an enormous relief as she told Ros about her past life. Her marriage, Auntie May's death, and the return to her beloved Greenways. Losing herself in the smallholding, and not bothering any more about Ray.

It was a good quarter of an hour before she stopped, events returning her to the present. 'So, you see, you were right when you suggested it was really my fault that he went off with your mother...'

Ros leaned across, putting a hand on hers. 'It was a cruel, thoughtless thing to say, and I wish I hadn't. Please try to forgive me.'

Anna sighed. 'Of course. But you did say it—and, in a way, I'm pleased. Hateful as the idea was at first, it made me begin to question myself. I know now that I'm not nearly as nice as I once thought I was. And I know, too, that I'm going to live very carefully in the future, especially when I meet—'

Her hands flew to her face in dismay. 'Oh, Ros, I forgot to tell you! I'm going to see your mother tomorrow.'

She bit off the words as she watched Ros's face grow taut and withdrawn, adding apologetically, 'How awful of me, I should have told you at once. She phoned earlier this evening, wanting news—she asked me to go and see her, to talk.'

She looked pleadingly at the girl. 'Ros, you

83

don't mind, do you? I mean, it won't make any difference to—to—' She broke off as she studied Ros's face, looking secretive and troubled.

Anna was furious with herself. She had spoiled everything, just when a lovely, warm rapport was beginning to grow between them. How could she have been so foolish, so self-centred, to let the news of Gilly's message drop out like that, casual and thoughtless?

Wretchedly, she waited for Ros to answer. When the reply came, it was so quiet she hardly heard the words. 'You can do whatever you like, it doesn't matter to me. If you feel you should meet my mother . . . well, good luck.'

An awkward silence stretched between them until Ros got up abruptly, avoiding Anna's watchful eyes. 'I think I'll go to bed. Thanks for listening for Tom. Good night . . .' She left the room without a smile, not looking back.

Alone, Anna felt a deep and miserable sense of bitterness sear the painful wound that had so recently just begun to heal.

❦

CHAPTER FIVE

The next day passed swiftly. With a baby in the house, there seemed no time at all in which to merely sit around thinking. Anna completed her usual morning routine—the washing, the shopping, the tour of inspection of the garden and the fields with Pete, the customary discussion between them, orders given, suggestions received—hardly remembering any of the conflict of the previous day.

It wasn't until after the midday meal that she really came face to face with Ros for the first time since breakfast. She had been anxious about their relationship after last night, but now Ros seemed carefree and friendly as she smiled, replacing the dishes on the big dresser.

'Getting ready for your visit to see Mum? I'd love to be a fly on the wall!'

'Why don't you come, too?' The suggestion was out before Anna could stop herself. She watched Ros's smile die, replaced by a cold severity that was out of keeping with the warm-hearted girl she thought she was slowly beginning to understand.

'No, thanks. I'm going to walk into the village with Tom.'

'But you don't have a pram.'

'I'll carry him. A sling's much better for babies, gives them direct contact with their mothers. Tom and I are going to really share his growing up.'

'Couldn't I—well, give you a lift there? And maybe pick you up on the way back?'

Ros faced Anna squarely, her gaze very direct and firm. 'Mrs Hoskins, please don't interfere. It's great of you to have us here, but I don't want to affect your life. We're fine, Tom and me. And we'll go our own way. If you don't mind . . .'

Put so definitely in her place, Anna could only smile rather grimly and nod agreement. She might have known. Young people were intent on leading their own lives these days. No more did they want to listen to outdated advice. And they had no use for parents or friends, either.

Sighing, she turned away. Maybe Ros's attitude was for the best. After all, there was no blood relationship between them. She was Ray's child, not Anna's. And Tom—that captivating, gorgeous baby—was nothing at all to do with her. She was merely someone giving him and his mother house room for as long as it suited Ros, and no longer.

Anna dressed carefully for her meeting with Gilly Leach, her sense of unhappy remoteness accentuated by those last forceful words with Ros. She mustn't get emotional. Mustn't over-react in any way. And, similarly, she must be matter-of-fact and firm at this approaching encounter.

Neat in a tweed skirt, blouse, and jacket, her hair newly washed and fluffy, with a touch of unaccustomed bright lipstick lightening her suntanned face, Anna left Greenways in the van, waving to Pete in the far field, and refusing to allow herself to wonder how far Ros and Tom had got in their journeying.

It took her nearly a quarter of an hour to drive to the suburb of the market town where Gilly Leach lived, and she drew up outside the small, semi-detached house a minute before three-thirty.

Walking up the short cement path, she looked at the orderly rows of summer annuals that nodded over the postage-stamp-sized lawn. Net curtains flickered for an instant as she rang the bell, and then, even as her stomach knotted in apprehension, the door opened and Gilly Leach stared into her eyes.

'Oh, come in, Mrs Hoskins. A lovely afternoon, isn't it?'

A cold smile lifted the painted mouth for an instant, and Anna awkwardly muttered something unintelligible about it being warm for the season as she followed her hostess into a bright, sunlit garden-room at the back of the house.

'I thought we'd sit here. Would you like to take off your coat? I'll put the kettle on...'

Gilly Leach was all manners and no warmth, Anna thought ruefully as she removed her grey jacket and slung it over the back of the grand cane chair Gilly had indicated. She felt dowdy and countrified in her years-old, pale-blue blouse and tweed skirt, compared with the other woman's elegance and good grooming.

High heels pattered out of the kitchen,

87

Gilly's pretty, printed, silk dress rustled gently and a tray of ornate china was set down on the table placed between two chairs. 'Milk?'

'Thanks. No sugar.'

'Dieting, like me, are you? One spreads as one gets older. Dreadful, isn't it?' Gilly handed over a teacup with an assessing, rather pitying smile, and within Anna the old, rebellious feelings quickly stirred.

'No, I don't diet. The work on the smallholding keeps me in trim. All that bending and stretching.' That would give the wretched woman something to think about! How could she expect to remain healthy and slim living such an indulgent lifestyle? Chocolate gâteau at three-thirty every afternoon? Ridiculous!

Suddenly, Anna felt better, more sure of herself. She drank her scented tea with renewed vitality.

'Mrs Leach—'

'Do call me Gilly. I'd like us to be friends.' This time the smile thawed a little and Anna paused doubtfully.

'Well—Gilly, then. And my name is Anna.'

'I know. Ray was always talking about you; he said you were a wonderful woman.' Gilly took a large mouthful of chocolate gâteau and delicately licked her cream-laden fingers.

Anna decided to plunge straight in. She wasn't one to use delaying tactics, or play subtle games. And if Gilly was ready to talk...

'If he thought I was so wonderful, then why did he take off and have an affair with you?' she asked bluntly, and saw Gilly's eyes widen for a fraction of a surprised second before quickly re-arranging her expression into the usual polite anonymity.

'You're very outspoken.' There was disapproval in the words, and Anna rose to the bait immediately.

'And about time, too. There's been far too much hidden in the past; you and Ray—and then Ros.'

Her feelings suddenly expanded, and she put down the cup, intent only on making Gilly understand how important it was to make up for what had gone before.

'Don't you see?' she urged, willing the other woman to do so. 'Secrets, all the way! And all of us hurt because of them.

'Well, it's taught me a lesson, I can tell you. I thought Ray and I were happily married...'

She stopped because it hurt, remembering times that had been happy, times before she devoted herself and her life to Greenways, times when she and Ray really had been fond of each other and easy in their relationship.

'You should have made him tell me, Gilly...' There was a tremble in her usually strong voice, and she stared over the tea-table with accusing eyes.

But, even after that upsurge of emotion, she was unprepared for the chilly, tinkling laugh

89

with which Gilly countered her attack.

'My dear Anna, surely you're the one who should have made it her business to know? Ray only came to me because he was cold-shouldered out of his own home. You offered no companionship, no understanding, no—'

Gilly paused delicately, brown eyes steely beneath the thick make-up. 'No warmth in your physical life with him. So what more obvious than he should look for it somewhere else? And you can't blame me for being able to give what you didn't even bother to think about ... He said you were a cold woman...'

There was unpleasant triumph in the stare that outgazed Anna, forcing her to look down at the empty plate before her. She felt guilty and unhappy. Even her anger, at having to accept the wretched pain that Gilly was inflicting, had died.

She could only agree with all that had been said. Cold, absorbed in the farm, no companionship, no understanding for the man who loved her. It was all quite true.

A silence grew between them until it broke into Anna's thoughts. Raising her head, she forced herself to meet Gilly's tight smile.

'He was right.' The words dragged out miserably, but Anna knew a slight sense of personal victory as she said them; at last she was facing the truth, agonising as it was. Now, perhaps, she could start building on that fact, making up for her deficiencies in the past.

Too late, of course, to say that she was sorry to Ray—she swallowed the hard lump in her throat and lifted her determined chin—but, even so, there must be some way in which she could make amends.

Out of the blue, she said spontaneously, 'I've learned so much about myself since—since I saw you, at his funeral. I know now that I was responsible for what happened, but I feel I'd like to make up for it by helping Ros. And the baby. After all, if Ray had still been alive, he would have wanted me to.'

'You have a damned nerve, Anna Hoskins!'

Anna blinked, staring at Gilly's suddenly-contracted face, hearing in the sharp, shrill rejoinder, a trace of hysteria and neurotic obsession.

'Why? What do you mean? What did I say?'

Gilly's hands fluttered as she put her empty plate on the tea-table, and her voice edged even higher as she snapped back, 'You come here, all smarmy and sorry for yourself, expecting to be forgiven for driving a man out of his own home, and then say he would have wanted you to take his child away from me—me, the one woman he really loved, the one who gave him everything that you were too selfish to offer! You're a terrible woman, Anna, and it's about time someone told you so!'

Anna began to tremble, but kept her voice even as she tried to put the matter into perspective. What had Ros said, about people
91

changing situations to protect themselves? How true that was—Gilly was doing it right now.

She drew in a deep breath. 'Look, I'm sorry you've been hurt. I'm sorry your daughter—' She checked herself abruptly. 'Ray's daughter, went off and got pregnant. I can imagine how dreadful that was for you.'

'It certainly was.' Gilly had regained control of herself. She sat back in her chair, her once-pretty face sullen as she relived the past. 'Ros and I were so close when she was small. Such a dear, biddable little girl, she was. And then, as she got older, all that business of discos and boy-friends, and not wanting to stay on at school, and take her exams. And her friends! Oh, I can't tell you the sort of ghastly young people she brought home—until I told her I wouldn't give them house-room any more.'

'And so she stayed away...' Anna's thoughtful voice was deep and quiet.

Gilly stared accusingly. 'You make it sound as if I tried to get rid of her! But I didn't. I simply said that if she wanted to go on living at home she must behave properly. I couldn't have that sort of rabble here, could I? In this quiet street? This is a nice neighbourhood, conventional, with good standards. What would everybody think if I had punks and layabouts coming to my house? No, no! I just told her that she must change her ideas.'

Anna looked pityingly at the tense face. 'But

she didn't...'

Gilly didn't answer. She bowed her head, shaking it slowly. Her hands lay knotted in her lap, and Anna thought she saw the afternoon sun gleam on falling tears.

She looked away, and thought humbly and understandingly about what she had been spared in her own life; the emotional conflict of having difficult children. For, even when they were beautiful and easy in their infancy, the chances were that they would grow up with different attitudes and aspirations, invariably bringing pain to their bemused parents.

'Gilly...' Her voice was gentle, and after a moment's pause the other woman raised her head wearily, blinking back the traces of tears, that had already smudged her mascara.

'Well?'

'You said, when I first came, that you felt we were going to be friends.'

Gilly sniffed disparagingly. 'What if I did?'

'I thought it was a stupid, unlikely thing to say then. But now—Gilly, do you think we might try? It would be so much better than going on with all this resentment and hate...'

*   *   *

Suddenly Anna discovered how important it was that Gilly should agree. A half-smile lifted her face. Who would ever have imagined that she, Anna Hoskins, strong and forceful, would

93

be pleading like this, waiting so anxiously for Ray's foolish and wronged mistress to reply?

It seemed an age until Gilly's face gradually cleared, and she raised her head a little higher. She pressed a scrap of handkerchief to her eyes and then finally managed a weak smile.

'I can't really see it working,' she said at last, 'but if you want us to try—well, all right. But don't expect too much of me. After all, I've been through such a lot, and all because of you...'

Anna pushed aside her quickly-rising anger. Recently, she had learned the hard way that one loved people in spite of their faults and funny ideas. Well, this proposed friendship with Gilly was going to be a test of that new understanding, and no mistake.

Cheerfully she reached across to pat the tightly-gripped hands that rested on the becoming silk dress, before she got to her feet, putting on her jacket as she did so.

'You're right. Let's see how things go, shall we? Now...' She glanced at her watch. 'I must go, I'm afraid. Pete—the boy who works for me—will be expecting his tea by the time I get back. And Ros, too.'

Gilly had risen to stand at her side, looking disapprovingly at Anna's work-stained hands as they fastened the buttons of her coat.

'How is Rosalind?' she asked stiffly. 'And the baby? A boy, they said at the hospital. What's she calling him?'

94

Anna smiled into the smudged eyes. 'Thomas Ray. Isn't that nice? He's such a lovely child. And Ros is fine. She had an easy delivery, and everything went fine. She's a born mother—' The words died as she saw, deep in Gilly's defensive brown eyes, a hint of pain that she could herself so easily identify with.

Carefully, she added, 'Ros may have been wrong, and I know you've been badly hurt, Gilly, but underneath it all, she does love you. If you could just bring yourself to accept that nowadays youth must go its own way—' But even as she finished, she knew she had gone too far.

Gilly's mouth drooped into the now familiar self-pitying expression. 'Don't tell me what I should or shouldn't do!' she said with exasperation as she turned away and headed for the front door. 'You say you want us to be friends, but in the next breath you start condemning the way I've behaved!' Holding the door open, she stared angrily at Anna, all her unhappiness clearly focused in an expression of indignant self-pity.

With a sense of relief, Anna stepped out into the warm, sun-kissed afternoon, seeking for the words that would put matters right, yet still show Gilly the way back to Ros's affections.

'Can I ask Ros to come and see you?' she said bluntly, hoping that such a direct question would force Gilly to see the unhappy situation more honestly.

Gilly's rosebud mouth worked nervously, and she stared down at the crazy paving of the path before she answered. Then she said abruptly, 'I don't mind...'

Suddenly her face flushed, and her eyes grew hard again. 'But if she's coming—well, she's got to behave herself, and look respectable. I'm not having her letting me down. Goodness knows what Edward will think when he sees her, all rags and tatters.'

'Edward?' Anna's mind raced. Then she remembered that Gilly, if not already re-married, was about to be so.

'My fiancé.' There was pride in the words, and Gilly's frown cleared as she smiled, all the tension released, her eyes clear and hopeful.

'How lovely for you. I hope you'll be happy.'

They looked at each other guardedly, and Gilly's eyes fell first. 'When I knew Ray wouldn't leave you I had to think about my future. I'm not a woman to live on my own. Edward is an old friend, we've been fond of each other for years.' She lifted her head almost defiantly. 'We get on very well.'

'I'm so glad for you,' Anna said gently. 'And I'm sure Ros must feel the same. I'll give her your message, and she can ring you to make arrangements for a visit.'

'Wait a minute!' Abruptly, Gilly ran back into the house, emerging again with her handbag, fumbling with a wallet as she did so. Drawing out two twenty pound notes, she thrust them upon Anna. 'Tell that daughter of mine to buy something decent to wear!'

Anna was delighted to hear the suspicion of humour as the words tumbled out. 'I don't want all that raggle-taggle wardrobe when she comes here. I mean, the neighbours—and Edward.'

Gilly looked at Anna with direct honesty, her eyes beginning to smile, and small patches of warmth making her face more human, more compassionate.

Deliberately, Anna folded the money and slipped it into her pocket. 'I'll tell her,' she said casually, and headed for the gate, where she glanced back over her shoulder. 'Thanks for asking me to come.'

She took a deep breath, calling upon all the back-sliding humanitarian feelings within her, and added, 'Maybe we'll meet again. Good-bye, Gilly.'

'Good-bye.' The thin voice sounded neither pleased nor affronted, and the hint of openness had already disappeared.

Anna drove off, feeling she was suddenly living in a vacuum, her emotions frozen and her mind incapable of understanding the extraordinary and unlooked-for situation into which she had stumbled.

*   *   *

Back at Greenways, she found Ros with Tom

97

in her arms, sitting in the mellow, late sunshine. Ros smiled as she got to her feet. 'Well, how did it go?'

Anna smiled warily, waiting until they were in the kitchen before replying. She removed her jacket and remembered the money burning a hole in one pocket. As she met Ros's curious stare she answered—'It might have been worse. We were very honest—both of us. We said things that needed to be said. It cleared the air a little, I think. But it wasn't easy. And—and—'

'And you didn't like her.' Such a flat statement made Anna meet Ros's direct gaze with a feeling of guilt. But she pushed the feeling from her. This was no time to be negative.

Her mouth lifted in a quirk of wry amusement. 'Not a lot,' she conceded dryly. 'And now I need a cup of tea. In my own thick, pottery mug. I've never liked bone china—or chocolate gâteau....'

She faced Ros. 'I'm sorry, but your mother and I are worlds apart. Her values aren't mine and never will be.' After filling the kettle, she held out the money Gilly had given her. 'She sent you this, Ros.'

Something made her withhold the condition of its use, but by the way Ros flushed and stared at the notes with an expression of acute distaste, Anna knew the girl understood all the same.

'For Tom? Or—or me?'

Anna sighed. 'For you, really. In the hope that you'll understand your appearance means a lot to her. She'd like you to look nice to meet Edward.'

'And the neighbours—all that curtain-twitching. Oh, God—' Ros hugged Tom to her, and buried her face in his small body. 'I don't want it. It's guilt money.'

Her voice was muffled, but Anne detected the bitterness, and leaned towards her, one hand smoothing the drooping hair.

'She's your mother, my dear, try and understand how she feels about you. She can't help thinking that appearances matter more than anything else. It's the way she was brought up.'

Abruptly, Anna's mind filled with the echo of Freddie's voice telling her so wisely that you shouldn't condemn people, but try to work out their motivations. A smile lifted her sombre face and when Ros, sighing, looked up, she let the smile continue, regarding the girl with affection and humour.

Ros cuddled Tom closer. 'I don't see anything funny about it all,' she said crossly.

Anna lifted the humming kettle and made the tea. 'You would if you were me,' she answered lightly. 'A sense of humour is a God-given gift. One should be thankful for it and keep it ticking over. Think about it, Ros.'

They drank in silence, punctuated only by

Tom's murmurs, but Anna felt that a growing rapport increasingly linked them. Although Ros had thrown the money to the floor, she no longer looked so unhappy or grim.

When Pete came in from the garden, kicking his boots off in the porch, Anna watched the smile that flowered to greet him. Ros was warm and welcoming, and bent to pick up the banknotes almost without thinking, as she sought Pete's returning smile.

Curiously, Anna wondered whether it was possible for a woman to love two men at the same time. As she left them chatting agreeably about the day's events, while she prepared the meal, it came to her that love was, in spite of all the poetic twaddle written and sung about it, a divisible quality.

She paused, peeling potatoes, her mind far away. After all, Ray had found it possible to love her and Gilly, too. So it became increasingly easy to accept that Ros could sit there so happily beside Pete, while Keith's baby stirred in her arms. Come to think of it, Anna conceded, she herself had also divided her love between Ray and Greenways.

And then, unbidden, Freddie's homely face swam before her eyes, and she grinned. Was she learning to divide it even further, she wondered, with humorous amazement.

*　　*　　*

100

The week sped along, days passing so smoothly and fast that it was Thursday again before Anna realised it. The heatwave had continued, serene and lovely, and the crops grew with happy abandon, untroubled by adverse conditions or pests.

Ros helped around the house, happily cooking when she had the chance, but mostly spending her time with Tom, and by now openly accepting that Anna would babysit for an hour each evening, while she and Pete were together. Listening to records, chatting, walking down to the village to have a drink at the pub.

Anna didn't ask questions, but saw how both Ros and Pete were blossoming as the relationship developed.

And then, inevitably, everything changed. First, the weather broke up, the sun retreating sullenly behind a bank of dark cloud, and occasional distant rumbles of thunder sending Ros running upstairs to her room with Tom in her arms, a flurry of skirts and hair, muttering about always having been scared of storms.

And on Thursday evening, Keith telephoned, his clipped, edgy voice seeming to Anna to break apart the easy atmosphere of the house.

'I'll be down for the week-end, OK, Mrs Hoskins?' he didn't give Anna a chance to say yes or no, but dashed on, words erupting down the line like a spitting machine-gun. 'Got a lot

101

to tell Ros—no, I can't stop to talk to her now...'

Just as well, Anna thought grimly. She didn't relish telling this pushy young man that Ros was out with Pete.

Keith gabbled on. 'Give her my love, will you? And say everything's turning out just great. See you, then. 'Bye!'

When, later, Anna delivered the brief message, she watched Ros's face very intently, and saw how the relaxed bloom instantly diminished.

Ros looked listless and a little lost, as she said tightly, 'I see. Sounds as if he's decided to turn into a devoted husband and father, doesn't it?'

She left the kitchen in a hurry, leaving Anna to ponder the words, not sure if they were said with sarcasm, or hopeful devotion.

In an endeavour to cover up the undeniable new sense of apprehension that now touched the waiting household. Anna invited Freddie to lunch on Friday.

She had been shopping in town, and so was able to put on a good spread. Ros had prepared salad, fresh from the garden, and the kitchen table supported quite a banquet as they all sat around it, their appetites already heartened by a glass of the wine which Freddie had donated.

'Well, here's to a good summer; a good crop of fruit and veg, eh, old girl? And, my word, if this salad is a sample of Greenways produce,

102

you're doing well already. You know, I thought your border looked brighter than usual this year, with all those annuals. Going to compete in the Flower Show, are you?'

Anna looked at his cheerful face, deeply grateful—trust Freddie to be there when she needed him most. She carved the ham joint and told him about her plan to enter the Cut Flower Class when the show took place in late July.

'Actually, I hope to win back from old Mother Pearson the silver cup that Ray gave when the Show first started; she's won it at least six years running ... goodness!'

Putting down the carvers, she stared blindly before her. 'I didn't realise it before—but I suppose that when Ray gave that cup, he was trying to do his bit with flowers and vegetables. He must have felt left out of things here ... and I didn't think—'

Ros broke into the suddenly emotional pause by saying quietly, 'So you've got to win it, this year. He would have liked that, I bet.'

'Yes.' Anna turned her head and looked into the girl's candid eyes. 'I'll do my best.'

Slowly, more general conversation began to murmur around the table. The wine flowed, the meal progressed, and by the time Anna had made coffee and taken it out into the rain-refreshed garden for a last relaxing ten minutes before resuming work, she felt the lunch had been a successful and friendly event.

Sipping her coffee, she listened to Freddie telling Ros about the various classes with the Flower Show programme. 'It's not just produce, you know—lots of arts and crafts, too. I always put in a couple of canvases. And one year Anna submitted a jumper she'd crocheted.'

He turned towards her, his smile warm, and she lazily recalled that she had done so. 'It was a sort of dusky pink—remember, Anna? And you pinned that nice old brooch of your aunt's on the collar. Won second prize, if I remember rightly. Jolly good effort.'

Anna saw Ros looking at her with fresh interest, and felt a sudden tug at her heart strings. That brooch—a ruby in an old-fashioned gold setting—would look good on Ros's print blouse.

Would she accept it? As a sort of commemoration of their meeting? Or Tom's birth? Heirlooms were meant to be passed on, and if one could manage it within one's lifetime, then the enjoyment could be appreciated and savoured.

She jumped up, smiling back over her shoulder as she ran indoors. 'Hang on—I'll go and get the brooch.'

Upstairs, she went straight to the little jewellery box where Auntie May had always kept her one string of pearls and the ruby brooch. The box was shabby, the clasp broken, but it was full of memories for Anna, and was precious.

She smiled as she opened it carefully, and then slowly her face fell as bewilderment dawned. 'It's not here...'

But she always kept it in the box on her dressing table. She never actually wore the brooch. She wasn't exactly a dressy woman, so there was no question of it being still pinned to a blouse or frock. So where was it?

Ten minutes later, having searched her entire bedroom, she went downstairs with one dreadful thought dominating her shocked mind. Was she cruelly jumping to unfounded conclusions?

The answer came with uncompromising directness. The brooch was worth something, the ruby unscratched, the setting twenty-four carat gold.

She had no knowledge of antiques—but there was one person who had been in the house lately who knew about such things. Who had, on his own joking admission, sold his own mother's heirlooms without her consent, and made a pretty penny from them.

Keith Turner. The name repeated itself continuously as she slowly returned to the garden feet dragging, her mind trying hopelessly to solve the problem of how to break the news to the happy faces that were already looking her way, smiling expectantly.

It was Ros's voice that reached her first, light as never before, full of interest, and what sounded like affection. 'Have you got it, Mrs Hoskins? I've always had a passion for old-fashioned bits and pieces. Do let me have a look...'

CHAPTER SIX

'It's gone—I can't find it anywhere!' Anna's upset tone of voice caused the smiles to fade. She turned from one perplexed face to the next, as if seeking their help.

'I always keep it in the same place. And I hardly ever wear it—I'm sure it hasn't been out of the jewellery box since I pinned it on that jumper, for the flower show. So where can it be?'

Within her the niggling suspicion that had become stronger and increasingly insistent as she ran downstairs suddenly exploded into speech. Almost without knowing what she was saying, she blurted out, 'You don't think that Keith...'

She stopped abruptly, as she took in the embarrassment and shock registering on the faces grouped around the table.

Freddie was frowning and shaking his head. Pete's usually sweet smile was gone, his clear eyes considering her accusation thoughtfully. And Ros—Anna's heart missed a beat—Ros was leaning across the table drumming her fists furiously as she snapped, 'How dare you? That's a rotten thing to say. Keith may not be all that reliable, but he's not a thief. Oh, you're just like Mum—you don't trust Keith, so you immediately condemn him...'

Knowing she was in the wrong, yet feeling an instinctive need to defend herself, Anna said feebly, 'I didn't actually say that, Ros.'

'But you thought it! Didn't you?' There was a long, painful pause while Freddie shuffled his feet and Pete got up, crossing to the window to stare out into the yard.

Ros's voice rang out again, demanding an answer. 'Didn't you, Mrs Hoskins?'

Her voice sounded uncertain as she met Ros's accusing eyes. 'Yes,' she admitted at last, and sat down heavily. 'Yes, I thought Keith might have taken it. I'm sorry, Ros, I shouldn't have said it, maybe not even thought such a thing. But—well—there it is.'

She sat up a little straighter, taking the full force of Ros's angry stare, and added bravely, 'I apologise. To you, and to Keith. Of course, the wretched brooch is lying around somewhere; it'll turn up quite unexpectedly and then I'll feel even worse than I do now. If that's possible.'

Her words hung in the air. Then Ros sighed, long and deeply, and lay back in her chair. She looked, Anna thought, touched and pained by her own vulnerability, as if she had all the cares in the world on her young shoulders.

'My dear—' Impulsively, she put out a hand to touch Ros's. 'Forgive me if I've hurt you. I—well—quite honestly, I didn't realise you felt so deeply about him.'

Ros slid her hand away and got to her feet without meeting Anna's concerned gaze. 'I didn't know myself,' she conceded in a muffled voice. 'That's the trouble you see—I'm not sure what I feel.'

She turned, and Anna saw her face crumple with impending tears. Then she left the room, the sound of her footsteps echoing through the quiet house as she clattered upstairs.

Anna felt the ensuing silence enveloping her. What had she done? If only she could recall those hasty, thoughtless words...

It was Freddie who broke the silence, making her look towards him, a smile on his face, a jest on his lips. Freddie, as ever, making the best of a bad job. 'Cheer up, old girl. Worse things have happened.'

She couldn't help smiling, near to tears herself, but grateful for his support. 'I suppose so. Oh, Freddie, what a thing to say! Why can't I learn to think before I speak? Poor Ros...'

To her surprise, it was Pete who chipped in then, his voice firm and direct. 'Don't blame yourself too much, Mrs Hoskins. I'd probably have said just the same thing in your place. I mean, anyone, can see what sort of chap that Keith Turner is.'

Anna stared, and Pete met her curious gaze

steadily. 'Well, he just uses people, doesn't he? Hasn't got any of the values I was taught when I was a boy; consideration, or caring about others. And look how he treated Ros—well, it speaks for itself. Mind you, I don't think he's a real criminal, but I bet if he saw something good lying about he'd make a grab. Stands to reason, doesn't it, a bloke like that?'

Anna felt foolishly encouraged for a moment—until Freddie said mildly, 'We've all done foolish things at some time, Pete. Can you say you've never taken anything that isn't yours?'

Intrigued, Anna watched Pete's face droop slightly, and he paused, unable to reply at once. Then his mouth tightened and he said, with a touch of unfamiliar and unbelievable primness, 'I wouldn't do any such thing, Mr Freeman. I know what's right and wrong, you see.'

'I'm glad to hear it. And don't you ever forget it, my lad. Just remember that temptation's often waiting round the next corner for all of us...'

For no reason that Anna could think of, Pete coloured, and then strode out of the room. She waited, hearing him putting on his boots at the back door, and then stared resentfully at Freddie.

'Why did you say that? Pete's always been open and thoroughly honest. You sounded as if you were accusing him...'

Freddie smiled matter-of-factly and began collecting the dirty dishes. 'Just trying to make him see both sides of the coin, love.'

*   *   *

Anna resolutely kept out of Ros's and Tom's way during the afternoon, and the work waiting for her in the vegetable field soothed her shattered feelings. Inside the fruit net, she filled the baskets with great juicy strawberries, enjoying their fragrance and beauty as she did so.

The garden was certainly productive this year; looking around, she saw, with immense satisfaction, that fruit had set firmly on the apple and pear trees, and that currants were already gathering colour as they swung on the bushes bordering the soft fruit plot.

Emerging from the net-enclosed area, she straightened her aching back and suddenly felt a great happiness—a sort of inner joy which transcended all the foolish worries about Ray and Gilly, Ros and Keith ... Anna's heart swelled and she closed her eyes, overcome by her feelings. Here, in the middle of a garden of growing things, with the sun hot on her face, her hands scarred and dirty from toiling in the earth, she knew herself to be blessed. Whatever misfortunes and anxieties might lie around the next corner, she would always remember, with gratitude and awe, this inexplicable and remarkable moment.

Then Ros appeared. She stopped abruptly when she saw Anna, looking for a moment as if she would turn back, but then slowly made her way towards the fruit cage. They looked at each other in silence, assessing, wondering, hoping.

Impulsively, Anna held out the loaded basket she carried. 'Have a strawberry—they haven't been weighed yet. Go on, they're delicious!'

The strain on Ros's face eased. A half-smile appeared, and she put the fruit into her mouth, mumbling, 'Mmm—gorgeous. What are you going to do with them all?'

Anna relaxed, as the smile grew. She led the way to the little outhouse where the weighing and packing was done. 'These are for the restaurant down the road. It's a regular order while the season's on. A good one, too—they pay very well.'

Ros watched keenly as Anna began sorting out the fruit into pre-weighed punnets. 'You need someone to help with this work. Couldn't you get a girl from the village? A teenager, perhaps?'

'I could,' Anna answered openly, 'but I can't afford to. You see, I run the place on a shoe-string, so I just have to spread myself a little thinner and cope with the extra work as it comes. I don't mind. I enjoy it.'

'Let me do it for you, next time—yes,

really…' the warmth in Ros's voice made Anna glance up. The eyes that uncannily reminded her of Ray were bright and keen and friendly, with a hint of concern only half-hidden.

Instinctively, Anna knew that Ros feared a rebuff, and she replied gently, 'That's great. It would be a terrific help and you could do it while Tom's asleep. Look, let me show you exactly what to do—and here's the invoice book and the ledger, for entering the bills up. I really appreciate this, you know, Ros.'

Their eyes met, almost shyly. Ros swallowed, and held the sleeping baby closer. Her voice shook a little.

'I'm sorry about what I said at lunchtime. And—this'll be a sort of thank you, too…'

Anna said no more. But, as she finished packing the loaded baskets into the back of the van, waving good-bye to Ros before driving down to Keeper's Cottage, she knew that some sort of powerful bond had been forged between them; a link created through a mutual love of the soil and miraculously welded by the invisible strength of family feeling.

'Anyone home?' When Keith's voice sounded outside the kitchen in the early evening, as Anna prepared the meal, she thought at once that he sounded glad to be back at Greenways.

'We're all here—come on in,' she called, firmly putting aside her lunchtime suspicions

112

and niggling feeling of hostility. She must be fair and open-minded. What had Ros said that had stung so badly? Something about hypocrisy and double standards. She smiled determinedly as he came through the doorway.

'Hello, Keith. You look tired—like a cup of tea?'

'Wouldn't I just. That walk up from the station must be at least ten miles.' He flung his bag down in the corner and walked up to Anna, where she stood scraping vegetables. 'Good of you to have me again, Mrs Hoskins.'

His brilliant eyes held hers for a moment and she felt almost weakened by the vitality and purpose they reflected. Bemused, she nodded, and went to the sink to fill the kettle.

'Sit down, Keith.' Slowly, she regained her composure and was able to pick up his jokey comment with equal lightness. 'Actually, the station's just over a mile away—you're obviously not a country boy.'

'I reckon cars are better than feet any day. Where's Ros? And young Tom?' Restlessly, he looked around the room and then towards the hall.

Anna's heart warmed to him. 'Upstairs. You might just catch your son before he drops off...' As he eagerly went up the stairs two at a time, she rebuked herself. What on earth was she doing, actually pushing him and Ros together? I must be mad, she told herself sharply. He's not the one for her. I'm sure he's not.

When they came down together a little later on, and she saw how Ros's smile had become bright and lovely, she was thankful that Pete had tactfully made excuses about not coming in to supper tonight. But, at the same time, Anna couldn't help wondering what Pete really felt about Keith's return to Greenway.

For a while, during the days when Keith was in London, she had almost thought that he and Ros were becoming very close. Oh, what a muddle it all was!

*   *   *

As the evening slipped by, she sat quietly, watching Keith's charm and magnetism bring out Ros's gaiety and warmth, and could only wonder at the workings of human chemistry. For Keith seemed almost a new person, even speaking in a quieter and less edgy way. And when he looked at Ros, Anna was held by the obvious depth of love in his eyes.

She made excuses to leave them together after the meal, saying she needed the empty kitchen to do her monthly accounts but, despite her concentration on the figures, she couldn't help being aware of their voices, talking so contentedly in the living-room.

Later Ros asked Anna to listen for Tom while she and Keith went into the garden. She saw them wandering idly in the dusky half-light, Keith's arm casually thrown around Ros's shoulders.

Anna finished her accounts and sat down, deep in thought. Was it possible she had been completely wrong in thinking badly of Keith? Was he simply a type she had never encountered before, and therefore was naturally prejudiced against? Certainly he seemed all sweetness and warmth this weekend—but could it last?

When Tom's first murmurs sounded through the house, Anna went to call Ros and then turned back, not caring to interrupt the embrace that brought two misty figures together at the bottom of the garden. A sudden thought occurred and she hoped Pete, returning from the village, wouldn't stumble across the lovers in the shadows...

But Ros must have heard her son's cries, for no sooner had Anna re-entered the house than she came running in. 'Tom's awake.'

Anna caught a quick flash of flushed cheeks and a glowing smile and felt more confused than ever, a feeling that deepened as she saw how tenderly Keith cradled his son in his arms, while Ros gathered together all the necessary baby paraphernalia.

It seemed a good idea to go to bed early and leave the little family alone. But not until Keith's quick footsteps crunched down the path, much later, and she knew he was heading for Freddie's bungalow and bed, did Anna allow herself to relax and finally sleep. For, despite the serenity of the evening, something inside her still felt wretchedly suspicious of Keith's easy charm and volatile manner.

She recognised the suspicions as well-founded when, with Pete's arrival next morning, fireworks began to erupt. The two men stared at each other across the kitchen as Anna handed around the usual eleven o'clock mugs of coffee.

'So you're back,' Pete remarked coldly, with an impersonal expression on his face. 'Couldn't keep away, eh? Too much smoke and hassle up there, I dare say. Nothing like the country for clean, honest living.'

Anna's heart jumped. Pete had paused slightly, emphasising the word honest, and his eyes flickered sideways to catch hers. What on earth did he think he was doing? She frowned and hurriedly cut thick slices of the fruit cake Ros had made yesterday.

'That's right,' she said, forcing gaiety into her voice. 'He's caught the country bug. Before you know it, he'll be as slow and lazy as we are.'

But the joke was lost. Keith had left his coffee untouched, crossing to Pete's side, chin lifted, knowing eyes gleaming with quick distrust.

'And just what's that supposed to mean? Honest, you said—'

'Keith—please don't—' Ros's voice was tight and shrill as she ran to put a hand on

116

his arm.

Shrugging it aside, he remained staring at Pete. 'Well? I'm waiting. That little word you made such a lot of just now needs a bit of explanation, I think.'

Horrified, yet feeling totally helpless, Anna watched doubt creep over Pete's face, and knew exactly what he must be thinking. He'd gone too far. He didn't want to actually accuse Keith of stealing that wretched brooch; had merely meant to needle him. He knew Ros would be desperately hurt if matters grew any worse, and he wouldn't want that to happen, not the way he felt about her...

With enormous relief Anna watched him lower his eyes, turn away to spoon sugar into his coffee, and say placatingly, 'Hey, don't get so worked up! So I chose the wrong word—well, I'm sorry. No offence meant.'

The tense silence lengthened until Anna felt at screaming point. She saw the increasing pallor on Ros's strained face and knew she must somehow bring this unpleasant moment to an end. Without further thought she stretched out a hand and knocked over her mug of coffee.

'Oh, dear, how clumsy of me. What a fool! All that mess—quick, Ros get a cloth, will you?'

The tension was broken. Ros mopped up the mess, and Anna put herself between the two men as she dealt with the soggy cake. She breathed deeply with relief and looked over her shoulder at Pete.

'I'll be along to help you with packing the lettuce in five minutes,' she said crisply, and watched him colour, unused to being ordered out in such a peremptory way. Too bad, Anna thought, still irritated at his thoughtlessness. He's as touchy as Keith is, in his own way. Well, he's got to learn like everyone else.

Once Pete had gone back to the garden, she looked across the room at Keith. 'Now—I'll thank you to keep your temper under control while you're here. This is my home, and I intend to keep it a peaceful one. Understand?'

Keith sat down, grinned up at her with a wry friendliness that made her words sound over-dramatic. 'I get you, Mrs Hoskins. You're the sort that shies away from confrontation aren't you? Not like me. I like to meet my problems head on.' Turning, he pulled Ros towards him. 'Come here, Ros. Shall we tell Mrs Hoskins our news?'

Anna's mouth opened in stunned surprise. She saw a certain nervousness veil Ros's answering smile as Keith's arm circled her waist.

'Stop it, Keith. It's not that important— well, not to Mrs Hoskins anyway.'

Anna's heart stopped for a moment, her thoughts racing. This was it, they were going to tell her that Ros was leaving, going away to marry Keith.

118

But, as she turned to look at Ros's serene, happy face, she knew she had to be ready for anything the girl told her.

'Don't worry, Mrs Hoskins.' Ros was smiling understandingly. 'It's just that Keith's found a way to bring his business down here. A friend is letting him use a holiday home he has vacant, and there's a double garage for storage. So Keith won't be too far away in future.'

* * *

Suddenly, Anna knew just how much this girl meant to her. Ros's happiness seemed more important than anything else—Keith's lack of morals, Pete's strange new secretiveness, even her own future, paled into insignificance as she watched the emotions slide across Ros's face.

Uncertainty was there, a hint of annoyance, too, no doubt because of Keith's crooked sense of humour. But warmth as well. A smile touched the girl's lips as Ros added wryly, 'He's talking about marriage, too—but I've said we'll wait and see.'

'Very wise of you.' Anna forced herself to meet Keith's knowing gaze. 'Don't rush into anything. Take the advice of someone who's learned the hard way, my lad. Oh, yes, you're right—I do avoid unpleasant confrontations, but only because I've discovered that discussion and compromise work better than brute force.'

119

He reached out to pat her hand, surprising her yet again with his quick change of mood and instinctive understanding. 'And no one's saying you're wrong.' Suddenly, he jerked to his feet. 'You know what, this country air's doing strange things to me! Nearly forgot something important, didn't I? Hang on—' He rushed upstairs and Anna looked at Ros curiously.

'What on earth—'

'He brought you a present. Me, too—look, isn't it lovely?' Ros pulled a fine gold chain from beneath her T-shirt, smiling proudly as she did so.

Anna broke off the uncharitable thoughts that formed in her mind and she spoke her next words gently, 'It's beautiful. Suits you, too.' Spontaneously, fired by the soft look in Ros's eyes, she added, 'He seems to care a lot for you, Ros—'

The girl drew in her breath sharply. The smile died, and she looked back at Anna with a return of the old timidity and indecision.

'Yes, I know. But—'

Then Keith was at the table again, jaunty as ever, putting an ancient, leather-bound book under Anna's nose. 'For you, only the best, Mrs Hoskins. My way of saying thanks for everything.'

Anna was speechless. Her hands crept out to explore the worn leather, with its gilt-tooled spine, to open the book and reveal old-

120

fashioned print. She gasped and looked up in amazement. 'Keith! It's an original Gerard! His herbal, one of the very first—oh, it's absolutely beautiful. My dear boy, what on earth made you do this?'

Immediately, she tried to cover up her embarrassment. 'I'm sorry, I shouldn't have sounded so surprised. I didn't mean to be so ungrateful.'

Keith's voice, unfamiliar in its quietness and depth, cut across her stuttering apology. 'Don't worry about it, Mrs Hoskins. I know it's an expensive present but—well, like I said only the best for you, Mrs Hoskins—after all you've done for Ros, and my Tom.'

For a while the room was quiet with a sense of shared contentment. Anna pored happily over the herbal, soaking up its old English charm and forgotten knowledge, her mind busy with the ideas that at once began to form. She'd always grown herbs, both for cooking and for the sheer enjoyment of their colours and fragrances, but now perhaps she might consider going into the commercial market...

Glancing up, she found Ros and Keith watching her with smiles that showed understanding.

Impulsively she said, 'Ros, we could start a real herb garden! The outlay's not huge, and there's that half-acre facing south, which has gone wild. I wonder—'

And then she bit her tongue. She saw Keith's

121

hand covering Ros's, and realised, too late, she was taking it for granted that Ros and Tom would always be here, at Greenways. For the moment, she had forgotten Keith completely.

What a foolish, self-centred fool she was. Again, she had fallen into the trap of others. Abruptly, she closed the book and pushed the new-born enthusiasm firmly away.

'I mean—' It was hard to come down to earth, but she forced herself more strongly than she would once have thought possible. 'I mean, of course, it's something I plan to do in the future. Pete can start clearing the ground in the autumn. No hurry about it.' She got to her feet, avoiding the eyes that watched so closely.

'Mrs Hoskins, it's a lovely idea, but—' Ros's words went unheard as Freddie's car rattled to a halt outside the back door, his beaming face drawing Anna towards him with immense relief.

'Oh, Freddie, how good to see you!' She planted an impulsive kiss on his cheek and was rewarded with the widening of his already broad smile.

'Nice to be wanted! Actually, I came to tell you how well young Keith did for me.' Freddie got out in his leisurely way and Anna noted, with an affection that surprised her, that his face was pink with sunburn, and that his checked shirt was daubed with lime-green paint. Trust Freddie to look his usual, reliable self.

Suddenly his words hit her. 'Keith?' she asked, surprised. 'What do you mean?'

Freddie leaned against his dirty car. 'Sold one of my pictures for twice as much as I expected, that's what. The one of Venus and the porpoises—remember it, Anna?' His face fell. 'Mmm—I don't think you liked it much. But the lad sold it. And I know just what I'm going to do with the cash, Anna...'

He was no longer the lazy, compliant man she always unkindly thought of as a doormat. Anna stared, seeing his face light up, sharpening the plain features into enthusiastic determination. What had happened to him to make him so different?

'I'm going to Florence to paint! Something I always longed to do as a penniless student, but couldn't. Well, the opportunity's here now—young Keith's sure he can go on selling my stuff, so I'll keep saving the pennies. Just think, old girl—a month or two in that wonderful city, all that art and history. I can hardly wait!'

His whole face glowed. Anna spoke then, more sharply than she intended, 'But I thought you were the stay-at-home type, Freddie—you've always said you were happy, here in your rut in the country.'

He sighed, a twinkle of mischief making his eyes dance. 'So I did, love. But I've changed. Anyone can change, you know! I'll go off without a care in the world!'

Anna realised she was staring at a stranger,

123

and her heart sank. In just a couple of minutes, Freddie had forgotten about his home and about her. She was left out of his dreams and plans, a nobody, who would stay at Greenways for ever, deep in her own rut, waiting for the occasional postcard from Italy, with its blue skies and elegant statuary, the carefree message saying, 'Having a lovely time.'

But—she caught her breath—would Freddie ever be wishing she was there? she wondered bitterly. And then it came to her that there was no reason why he should need her any longer; for years she had merely made use of him, and now, finally, he had discovered the way to a new life.

She would miss him—abruptly, she knew just how badly—but she couldn't blame him for grabbing the golden chance. And somehow she must try to be happy for him.

*   *   *

As if he read her thoughts, Freddie's smile died. 'Sorry, I'm going on a bit. Of course, nothing's settled yet. All right, are you, Anna? You're looking a bit peaky...'

His concern ruffled her even further. She swung away, saying edgily, 'I'm fine, thanks. But I'm busy. Go and talk to Ros and Keith. They've got nothing else to do.'

Halfway towards the lettuce field, she wished she hadn't snapped like that. What on earth had come over her? It was all because of Keith—giving her that book, setting her off making impossible plans. And then Freddie—yes, that was Keith's doing, too. Selling that ghastly picture, building up Freddie's stupid dreams. And Ros...

Anna stopped at the packing shed to collect a knife and a pile of boxes, seeing Ros's face in her mind's eye. Ros, uncertain, vulnerable, being torn first one way, then the other—again, all Keith's fault. Now, if only Ros could choose to love Pete...

Anna joined Pete and together they harvested the lettuce crop that must be driven to market before noon. They worked in silence, and, for the first time in years, with a feeling of uneasiness between them. During that hot, back-aching hour of cutting and packing, Anna's thoughts ran riot, and by the time she wearily saw Pete drive away with the boxes safely stowed in the van, she had come to a more perceptive state of mind.

Now she knew just how Gilly Leach must feel, alone and neglected. Compassion came fast, disturbing in its clarity, and after the midday meal, when she had seen Ros, Keith and Tom go off on a trip to the nearby shady woodland, Anna knew exactly what she had to do.

Gilly's quite voice answered her telephone call at once. Anna wondered wryly if Gilly had been sitting there, all dressed up, waiting for

125

the bell to ring.

It was a sad picture she conjured up, making her more sympathetic than ever as she exchanged greetings, and then asked, 'Would you like to come over and see Ros and the baby, Gilly?'

At first, Gilly sounded uncertain, but it was obvious that she dearly longed to come. Anna guessed that she needed support before meeting her erring daughter and new grandson.

'Bring your fiancé with you,' Anna heard herself say.

'Edward? I don't know. But perhaps . . . well, all right. It would be better than Rosalind coming here, I suppose.'

'Good,' Anna enthused, glad to hear the ring of excitement in Gilly's voice. 'I'll expect you on—shall we say, Monday afternoon?'

She replaced the receiver, feeling proud of her move. By Monday Keith would be back in London, and Ros probably a little lonely without him. A most opportune time for Gilly to call. But, of course, nothing must be said until the very day. Anna smiled rather nervously as she imagined what Ros would say if she knew in advance.

First, though, there was the week-end to get through. It was impossible to keep Pete and Keith apart, Anna realised, as Sunday dawned, and she thought back over the numerous little scraps and skirmishes that had marred the family atmosphere since Keith's return on Friday evening.

And Pete was as bad as Keith in stirring up trouble. What had happened to his usually tolerant nature? Anna wondered, with growing annoyance. There was that nasty business on Saturday morning, and then today, having a cup of tea outside on the lawn, Keith had started needling Pete, as if to get his own back.

'Always been a gardener have you, then?'

Pete, sitting on the grass beside Tom's carry-cot, had stiffened immediately at the arrogant tone of voice. 'I've done other jobs in my time.' He sounded defensive.

Anna had caught Ros's eye. They exchanged wary glances, and Anna realised just how much Ros hated this seemingly interminable wrangling.

Keith's voice was light, but deprecating. 'Such as what? Can't see you doing a real job—not one that takes any brain power. Stands to reason, friend.' The last word somehow made the rudeness even more offensive.

Pete coloured and slowly shifted his long legs. 'I'm not stupid. Even if I do work on the land I have feelings, just like other people. But I wouldn't expect a gold-digger like you to know about such things—'

Anna slammed down the teapot and glared at them both. 'Stop it!' she demanded. 'You're like a couple of small boys.' She saw Keith's

127

grin widen, saw Pete frown, and felt more irritated than ever. 'Surely you're both old enough—and sensible enough—to see how ridiculous you're being? Ros and I are absolutely fed up with all this carry on...'

Then she wished she hadn't brought Ros into it. Both men abruptly looked at the girl and Pete, getting to his feet, towering over Keith in a semi-belligerent way, said quietly, 'Then perhaps Ros would like to do something about it. I mean, it's up to her, isn't it?'

Ros looked up, from one tense face to the other, her eyes growing desperate with indecision. Then the becoming glow of suntan, which had given her such a healthy appearance lately, faded. She lowered her gaze.

'Stop it, Pete,' she muttered. 'You're not helping much.'

Keith stretched in his chair, then put out a possessive hand to stroke her hair. 'No, Pete, you're not helping at all. Don't you think it's time you got back to work?'

Anna took in a deep breath, ready to explode, but Pete forestalled her. He ignored Keith's quick sarcasm and smiled gravely down at Ros.

'I'm sorry,' he said, his voice very low. 'I didn't mean to make things worse.'

They all watched in silence as he went out of the garden and back to the day's hoeing of the vegetable field. Then Keith pulled Ros to her feet.

128

'Come on, Ros let's take Tom for a walk ...'

Ros looked uncertain, but then she nodded and Anna sat watching as the two figures set off, pushing the pram in front of them.

Anna sat on in the empty, gloriously-peaceful garden, busy with her thoughts. She sighed as she wondered how Ros would react to Gilly's visit tomorrow. Had she been foolish to invite her? Well, too late now; perhaps it might even help matters. Once again, on Monday, Anna took Keith to the station.

'Thanks a lot.' He pecked her cheek. 'See you next Friday—OK, Mrs Hoskins?' Then he ran for the train, glib words running around her head, cheery smile bright before her eyes. To her Keith was an unknown quantity and she had to leave it at that.

Back at Greenways, Anna found time to vacuum the living-room and cleverly persuade Ros to make one of her special strawberry shortcakes.

Lunch-time was serene without Keith and Pete's clever remarks spoiling the atmosphere. Ros was quiet, but not unhappily so, and when Pete hesitantly asked if she'd like to go down to the village after supper to watch a local cricket match, she said yes immediately.

Only as Anna finished the washing up, and was wondering how she could prevent Ros from leaving the house during the afternoon, did the trouble start.

Ros put the last dish neatly on the dresser

and then turned around, her eyes large and serious, looking at Anna as if she had just arrived at a momentous decision.

'Mrs Hoskins...' Her voice was quiet, but very determined. 'Please don't think me ungrateful. I shall always remember how you took me in—me and Tom—but...'

Anna felt her feet turn to stone. She stood by the door, about to go upstairs and change from jeans into a skirt, ready for Gilly's expected visit, and was suddenly caught by the impending knowledge of what Ros was trying to tell her. A knot of anxiety twisted inside her.

'I'm going away, Mrs Hoskins, with Tom. Just us, on our own. I need time to sort it all out, you see.'

'But—' Anna was worried for the girl even though she understood how she felt. 'Where will you go? Oh, Ros, please don't—please stay here, where you're both safe and loved.'

Ros sighed and smiled a little wearily. 'Don't you see? I can't spend the rest of my life being safe. I have to take risks, make my own future.'

Anna panicked. 'I won't let you go!' she shouted and then stopped as Ros's usually gentle expression grew hard and cold.

'That's all I need,' she ground out. 'You sound like my mother, and she's the last person in the world I need at the moment.'

'Ros, Ros!' Anna was distraught. She knew she had spoiled everything. Now Ros and Tom would leave, probably she'd never see them

130

again. She saw Ros move quickly towards the open back door and went to her, trying desperately to make amends.

'Oh, my dear, I'm sorry—I didn't mean—'

'Leave me alone!' Ros vanished into the yard.

Anna halted in the doorway, feeling suddenly old and exhausted, and saw, with her heart sinking, that the situation was even worse than she had imagined.

An immaculate, silver-grey car was parked in the yard, and Gilly, elegant in dark green silk, had already got out, followed by a tall, distinguished-looking man.

Ros paused in her wild flight, suddenly cornered by the newcomers. Anna saw her put a hand to her mouth, heard her voice choke as she cried furiously, 'Mum! Oh, no! Who told you to come here?'

CHAPTER SEVEN

Anna, seemingly turned to stone in the kitchen door-way, watched Gilly Leach's face go bright pink, before turning to a pale, washed-out grey colour.

'Rosalind!' she said unevenly. 'Rosalind—I thought you'd be glad to see me . . .' Her gloved hands reached out for Ros, who shied away, looking desperately around her for a chance to run. But the tall man was walking from the car on one side, her mother stood on the other.

Anna swallowed the painful lump in her throat and reluctantly advanced from the doorway, effectively cutting off the last escape route.

This was a terrible situation, and it was all her doing; but a meeting between Ros and Gilly was inevitable, and Anna had a feeling somehow that this was the right moment.

Not that it seemed so. Cornered, Ros pulled back from Gilly's trembling hand. 'Go away!' she said angrily. 'I don't want anything to do with you! You turned me out when I needed you—well, now the tables are turned!'

'But, Rosalind, dear...'

'Go home, Mum! Let Edward take you back where you belong. Because you're not welcome here.'

Anna's heart thudded, but she stepped forward bravely, saying in a low voice, 'This is my house, Ros, not yours, and it's for me to say who can and can't come here. And as I personally invited your mother—'

'You did what?' Ros's eyes were wild, like a trapped animal, and just for a second Anna wanted to back away. But then she thought of Ros's tendency not to let loose the bottled-up anger and hurt that the past had caused her. Perhaps it was just as well that Ros was letting it all spill out now.

So, lifting her chin determinedly, Anna

132

forced herself to look straight at Ros. 'I told you. I asked your mother to come,' she answered as lightly as possible. 'She's been longing to see you and the baby. Tom is her grandson, after all.'

As she had hoped, the mention of Tom's name brought a measure of sense to Ros's thoughts. She looked uncertainly from Anna to Gilly, and back again. 'Tom,' she muttered and then, turning, glanced up towards the open bedroom window. 'I hope we haven't wakened him.'

Quickly, Anna said, 'I thought I heard him a moment ago.' Smiling reassuringly, she willed Ros to regain her lost composure by concentrating on the child. 'Why not bring him down if he's awake?' she suggested. 'And I'll make the tea. I'm sure we could all do with a cup. Now, Gilly—do come in. That's right. In here...' She gestured towards the sitting-room door.

Anna held her breath as she settled her guests down, not relaxing until she heard Ros at last go upstairs, not in a temper, but slowly and controlledly, to bring Tom down.

Somehow Anna kept up a friendly, trivial conversation. She talked about the house, her happy years there, the weather, the excellent crop of strawberries.

'Strawberry shortcake? It's years since I tasted any,' Gilly murmured, still looking pale and distressed, sipping her tea as she toyed

133

with the cake.

'Try a piece,' Anna said casually. 'And you, Mr—er—'

'Edward Grainger, Mrs Hoskins. A little late for formal introductions, I'm afraid, after everything that's happened...'

Anna caught the smile in the man's clear, grey eyes as he sat very close to Gilly on the couch, obviously ready to give whatever support was needed.

Anna liked him on sight. For all his conventional lifestyle—his smart clothes, the expensive car—she instinctively knew his heart was in the right place. He understood Gilly's nervous, capricious ways and, from the way he'd smiled at Ros, irate as she was, he looked as if he could easily cope with any family squabbles.

'I'm delighted to meet you, Edward. And I'm Anna...'

The atmosphere was improving. Anna relaxed a little and looked across at Gilly, who was eating her shortcake with evident enjoyment. Delicately brushing a crumb from her mouth, she met Anna's eyes and managed a brief smile.

'Beautiful cake,' she said appreciatively.

Anna jumped at the opportunity the comment offered. 'Your daughter made it,' she said bluntly. 'She's an excellent cook. You should be very proud of her talent.'

For a moment Gilly just stared, her face

falling once again into the familiar droop of despair. 'I didn't know,' she said in a very low voice. 'Didn't know she could even boil an egg. I—I don't know much about her, do I? Not really. She's my daughter, but—she's more like a stranger—'

Gulping, she hid her face in a scrap of lace handkerchief and turned to Edward. 'I've been such a fool. Such a bad mother.'

'Now, now, don't let's have any more scenes, love. Cheer up.' He patted her hand with a touch of fond authority.

Obediently she stopped sniffing, looking up gratefully.

Uncomfortably watching the little drama, Anna was struck by the expression of devotion on Gilly's tear-stained face. 'Let me fill your cup,' she said to Gilly, slightly embarrassed.

Then there was a step on the stairs, and they all looked up to see Ros come into the room carrying Tom.

She stopped short of the tea-table, staring at her mother with a very determined face. 'This is Tom,' she said flatly, 'His full name's Thomas Ray Leach. I'm going to register his birth tomorrow.'

Her face was flushed, but Anna saw that the anger was gone, and that she was now able to look at Gilly without any sign of temper. Her next words made Anna sigh with relief.

'I'm sorry I said all those rotten things. But I didn't expect to see you. And—and you've come at the wrong time. You see, I was just leaving.'

Gilly gaped. 'Leaving? Where are you going?' Her thin voice rose petulantly. 'I don't understand.'

'Perhaps we should have some more tea, and some of Rosalind's excellent shortcake,' Edward put in tactfully.

Anna seized the opportunity to pull up a chair. 'Sit down, Ros. You have a cup, too. I'll hold Tom, shall I?'

'No!' Ros turned on her sharply. 'No one's going to take Tom. He's mine.'

'I didn't mean—'

'I can't trust anyone! Not even you now, Mrs Hoskins.'

Anna sat back, feeling chilled, and watched Ros push away the cup of tea she had just poured.

Gilly was staring at Tom with undisguised longing in her brown eyes. 'What a beautiful boy—may I hold him?'

Ros snatched him closer to her body. 'No, you can't. You'll treat him like you treat me— you'll just use him and then turn him out when he does something you don't like...'

'Oh, Rosalind, I didn't do that! It was you, being so difficult, so unco-operative.' Gilly's voice was shrill and tearful. 'I loved you, but I couldn't cope with your rebellious ways. It seemed better that you should go and do what you wanted—believe me, I wasn't being hard

136

or selfish. I only wanted what was best for you.'

In the silence the followed Gilly's impassioned words, Anna heard the back door click open and steps cross from the kitchen into the hall. Not quite sure whether to welcome the intruder, or turn him out, she looked over her shoulder to see Pete standing in the doorway, calmly assessing the situation.

'Though I heard raised voices,' he said quietly. 'Everything OK, Ros?' His eyes shifted from one outraged face to the other.

Ros gulped and put out her free hand to touch Pete's. 'Not really,' she admitted unevenly. 'I'm glad you're here.'

Gilly drew herself up, staring at Pete with critical, unfriendly eyes. 'And who's this?' she asked offensively. 'Tom's father? Or just one more of your friends?'

Anna gasped, looking at Pete, ready to try to stop the forthright response she guessed he would make. But there was such a hint of cynical amusement on his sun-tanned face that she kept silent. It dawned on her that Pete, better than any of them, knew the best way to cope with this dramatic, unpleasant scene.

Ros's eyes snapped furiously at her mother. 'That's an awful thing to say! What do you think I am, Mum?'

Pete's good-humoured voice cut across hers with lazy reassurance. 'It's OK, Ros. Your mother never met Keith or me, so I suppose it's a fair question. As for the rest of it—well...'

Very deliberately he smiled at Gilly, and put out a large, earth-engrained hand.

'I'm Pete Lazenby and I work here at Greenways. I'm very fond of your daughter Mrs Leach, and, although Ros doesn't know what she wants from her future yet, I'm hoping I figure in it somewhere. It's good to meet you at last.'

Gilly looked stunned. Her mouth dropped open, and she stared at Pete's hand for a long moment before Edward came to the rescue.

'Come along, dear—you're keeping the young man waiting, and a hard-working hand like that is probably itching to get on with the next job!' The humour in the words made Gilly blink.

'Oh. Yes, of course.' She touched Pete's fingers grudgingly. 'How do you do...' And immediately wiped her own hands on her handkerchief.

Cheerfully, Pete said, 'I won't stay. I'm in the middle of hooking down some nettles, but I wanted to meet you Mrs Leach. Wanted you to know who I am. We'll meet again, I'm sure.'

'Have some tea while you're here, Pete?' Anna caught his eyes as he crossed the room, with a last, swift smile at Ros.

He glanced over his shoulder. 'Well—'

Ros moved fast. On her feet, she said, 'I'll get it,' and then leaned over to dump the baby in her mother's unprepared arms.

'Here you are, Mum. Look after Tom for

me, please.' She followed Pete into the kitchen, and Anna heard the door latch behind her.

Realising just how tense she had been until this moment, Anna gladly relaxed and helped herself to some shortcake. I've earned this, she told herself wryly, and then caught Edward's amused eye, and knew he was sharing her thoughts.

With the arrival of the baby in her arms, Gilly had snapped out of her self-pity. Suddenly, as Anna watched, she became softer, less conscious of herself, much more like a grandmother with her first grandchild.

'Tom,' she said gently. 'Tom. Yes, you look like a Tom. There, now, don't cry—I'm your new grandmother. You and I have to get used to each other.'

She arranged the baby more comfortably on her lap and smoothed his fly-away hair. Tom stopped grizzling and stared up at her, clearly fascinated by the movement of the bright beads around her neck.

'He's smiling. Look at him—he's smiling at me.' Gilly turned jubilantly towards Edward, who nodded dutifully.

'So he is. And why not? He's going to love you, my dear. This is just the beginning of a long and happy relationship, I'm quite sure.'

Anna could feel a lump rising in her throat. There was something terribly touching about Gilly's amazed joy in seeing her grandchild. Anna thought back to her own moment of emotional revelation when she had first seen Ros with young Tom, and knew exactly how Gilly must be feeling.

Then a wave of bitterness swept through her, and she was, for a second, envious of the other woman's legal claim to the child.

But, slowly the jealousy faded, for she was learning now never to allow a moment to pass without becoming aware of its potential for happiness. So she tried to share Gilly's joy, and felt all the better for persuading herself to do so.

After all, she was lucky to have had the chance of taking care of Ros and Tom as she did. Just supposing Ros had never come to Greenway? Anna imagined a future without even that short memory, and it made her shiver.

In the kitchen, the hum of faint voices died, and the back door slammed. Ros returned to the living-room, smiling thoughtfully to herself, Anna noticed, and her eyes immediately went to Gilly. Anna sensed the girl's longing to take Tom back into her own arms, but saw, too, how Ros finally decided to leave him where he was.

Sitting down, she looked across at her mother. 'He's taken a fancy to you, Mum.'

'Yes,' Gilly agreed, her voice softened by the smile that spread across her lips. 'He's—oh, Rosalind, he's such a lovely boy!'

Suddenly she glanced up, meeting her

140

daughter's eyes, then held out the bundle of cooing baby. 'Thank you, dear, for letting me share him. Maybe we'd be able to make it a more permanent thing. I mean, there's plenty of room in the house, and—and—'

Ros hugged Tom to her, and Anna saw the old, withdrawn look slip back across her face. 'No,' she said bluntly, 'Tom and I are going off on our own. I've got a lot of things on my mind. I need to be away from everybody.'

Silence lengthened, and Anna felt a return of animosity between mother and daughter. Gilly's face was set again, and she sat stiffly, no longer the maternal figure that had softened so becomingly at the baby's helplessness.

'I see. Well, of course, you'll do whatever you want. So nothing has really changed, has it?' Her brittle voice tailed off and she got up, smoothing her skirt, patting her faultlessly groomed hair, finding her handbag and glancing down at Edward for support. 'Time we went home, I think ...'

He rose to the occasion, and Anna noticed with admiration how his smile accepted Gilly's ungraciousness. 'Just as you like, my love.' He looked at Anna and nodded courteously. 'Thank you for your generous hospitality, Anna. So good of you to have asked us to come today.'

The warmth of his words eased Anna's tension, but she saw Ros's thunderous face, and knew with a sinking feeling that she wasn't forgiven yet for inviting them.

Outside, the guests headed for the car, with Anna following and Ros and the baby leaning against the open doorway. There was a figure lurking in the shadow of the garage, and Anna saw Pete watching, unnoticed by everyone except herself.

Gilly got into the car, head erect, not looking at anything except the windscreen in front of her as Anna said good-bye, but Edward, to her great relief, crossed the yard to Ros who stood there, unsmiling. He put his hands on hers as she clasped the baby and looked down very warmly into her sullen face.

'Come and visit your mother some time, my dear. She's as obstinate as you are . . .' His smile flashed out, robbing the words of all offence. 'But I know she'd love to have you—for a few days, a few weeks—as long as you care to stay. And I think you'll find things will change between you, with give and take on both sides. Come to our wedding next month, won't you? We'd love to have you. And young Tom, of course.'

Without waiting for a reply, he strode back to the car, where Gilly was once again pressing her scrap of handkerchief to her eyes. Edward drove out of the yard, with a last smile for Anna and raising a hand in salute to Pete, hovering by the garage.

Anna turned then to look at Ros, who met her eyes with an expression of uncertainty and reluctant surprise. Anna gave her opportunity to speak.

'Don't say anything,' she urged. 'I know how you feel—that you resent any interference—but I only did what I knew had to be done. Blame me, if you must, I expect I'll get over it. Well, now I'm going to do some work. I feel as if I need to be back among the plants. At least they don't complain or bear any grudges.'

It was the nearest she had ever come to letting Ros know just how deeply she felt about the unhappy situation, and, although the look on the girl's face stayed with her as she changed her clothes and then walked off towards the vegetable field, she knew she had been right to give expression to her personal indignation and pain. Ros must learn that it wasn't possible just to live for yourself alone.

She was in the tool shed, preparing herself for a welcome couple of hours' hoeing, when she heard Pete's voice and realised he had gone across to the kitchen doorway to talk to Ros. Now it was Anna's turn to hover in the shadows, just as he had recently done, while she listened to the voice that rose and fell within easy earshot.

'You were a bit hard on your mum, love.' Pete sounded understanding, but serious, and Anna realised, with a shock of awareness, just how close he and Ros had become. She listened for Ros's grudging reply.

143

'Don't you start on me, too. I've had enough for one day. Oh, Pete, I thought you understood...'

Uncomfortably, Anna wished she could leave the shed without being seen. Obviously, they had both forgotten she was there. Well, she had no inclination to eavesdrop, but if she came out now they would both know she had been listening, and the situation would only become more involved.

No doubt Ros would blame her for this, too; there seemed no option but to remain hidden, forced to overhear a private conversation against her will.

'I do understand. You know I do. We've been through all this before, and I realise your mum made life hard for you. But can't you see now that she's just aching to make up and start again? Ros, you're so lucky to have a mother—don't play games with her. Can't you imagine how you'd feel if young Tom told you where to go, one day in the future?'

Anna's emotions began to rise. How right he was to try to persuade Ros to forgive Gilly's thoughtlessness and lack of proper parental common sense. Surely Ros must see that what he said was just the plain truth? But her heart sank again as Ros's hurt voice flung a last answer back at him.

'That's a rotten thing to say! You know that I'll always do whatever's best for Tom. Not like Mum, who—'

144

'Who thought that she was doing the best for you. Think about it, Ros...'

In the silence that followed, Anna found himself praying hard that Pete's commonsense would make Ros see reason. But when Ros finally spoke, she sounded full of the old self-pity and sullenness.

'It's hopeless. Keith goes on at me, Mrs Hoskins, too—and now you. Well, I'm off. No, Pete, don't try to stop me...'

There was a sound of hasty footsteps retreating, and then Pete's voice, heavy with disappointment. 'I won't stop you, love. You've got to sort this thing out on your own. But let me at least suggest somewhere for you and Tom to stay. Remember we met Stevie and Dawn at the pub last week? They've got a place in Somerset—well, I know Dawn would have you. She works all day, so you'd be virtually on your own. And—and I'd know that you and Tom were safe.'

Anna's hopes rose, only to be dashed again as Ros said crossly, 'No. I'm sorry, but it wouldn't be any good. We'd chat and I'd ask advice, and then I'd be back to square one. Pete, I've got to handle this decision alone. Try to see it my way, please?'

'I do.' He sounded resigned. 'When are you going?'

Anna could restrain herself no longer. Ashamedly, she came out of the shed and went across the yard to meet the startled faces that

145

stared accusingly at her.

'I'm sorry,' she said. 'I didn't mean to eavesdrop, but—'

'You heard us?' Ros looked furious.

Anna tried to pacify her. 'Yes, I did. You see, I was in there, and then Pete started talking, and I felt I couldn't come out in the middle of his speech.'

'It's OK, Mrs Hoskins.' He gave her a benevolent smile, and she felt ridiculously like a small child forgiven by a kindly schoolmaster for some stupid prank.

'If you really must go, Ros—' She turned to meet Ros's obvious disapproval, and smiled pleadingly at the withdrawn face, the expression in such direct contrast to that of the baby sleeping so peacefully in her arms. Anna stumbled on. 'I'd like to give you some money. You must have somewhere to stay ... And for train fares ... And things for Tom ...'

Her feverish words slowly petered out, for Ros was returning her stare with plain dislike. Her eyes glinted fiercely as she muttered. 'All you can think of is money and material things. Just like my mum.'

'No, that's not true!' Anna burst out suddenly, her anguish beginning to overflow. 'It's because I love you, and Tom, that I'm so worried. Can't you possibly try to understand how I feel?'

She met Ros's abruptly startled eyes and added wretchedly, 'No, of course not. Why

146

should you? I don't suppose you've ever really loved anyone, have you? Not until you had Tom. So how can you even hope to know how I feel?' Her voice broke, and she knew tears weren't far away.

It was Pete's reassuring hand on her shoulder that broke the desperate tension of the scene. 'Mrs Hoskins, don't say any more. Ros needs time on her own to think things over. She's sensible, she won't come to any harm—not now she's got Tom to look after.'

Anna stared up at him, amazed by the conviction in his words, and the expression of relaxed tolerance on his face. From deep inside her came, once again, that anguished wish that he were her son—how wonderful it would be to have a young man like Pete to be proud of. Bowing her head, she nodded, accepting what he said.

She left them alone in the yard, turning her face so that no one would see the threatening tears, and went to the sunny field beyond the gate, where a tangled sea of unhoed pink bindweed awaited her attention.

The hot silence slowly worked upon her tense muscles and mind, and the earthy fragrance of the freshly-hoed soil at least brought a measure of balance to her churning thoughts. By the time she had finished for the day she was able to return to the house and face its emptiness; for, true to her words, Ros and Tom had gone.

Although Anna had accepted the inevitability of their departure, some lingering sense of yearning for human contact made her go into every room. It was foolish and unnecessary, and when she returned to the kitchen her heart had grown heavier than before.

There were so many reminders of Ros and Tom which, in their absence, had swelled into stabs of increasing pain. The smell of talcum powder in the bathroom, a forgotten shawl dangling over the back of a chair...

Wretchedly, Anna set about preparing the evening meal, but even that had its memories, for now there was only herself and Pete to cook for.

When Pete arrived, her nerves were at snapping point, and she glared at him, hating the expression of acceptance on his face.

'I'm worried to death,' she burst out. 'How will Ros manage? Pete—we must find her and bring her back.' Suddenly her face brightened, and she turned away quickly, heading for the hall. 'Of course! Why didn't I think of it before? I'll phone at the police—they'll find her easily enough, and then—'

But Pete was at the telephone before her, his hand covering the instrument as she reached out to lift the receiver.

'No, Mrs Hoskins,' he said, with a finality that made her step back. 'That would only make things worse.'

'But—' Anna's mind was suddenly bristling with ideas; she must find Ros, must bring her home. 'I'll tell Keith! I mean, he has a right to know where his child is.' She bit off the words as a stubborn look spread across Pete's normally good-humoured face.

'That's ridiculous. Tom is perfectly safe with Ros. She is his mother, after all.'

Anna's face flamed at the rebuke. 'Of course, I know that! And I'm not saying that she won't look after him, but ... well, shouldn't we at least tell Mrs Leach? Surely someone ought to know that Ros and the baby have gone?'

Pete sighed, and a resigned twinkle appeared in his dark eyes. He led Anna gently back towards the kitchen.

'Let's have tea, Mrs Hoskins. There's nothing either of us can do until Ros makes up her mind about her future. It's difficult, I know, to go on as if nothing has happened, but to be fair, that's what we have to do.'

Anna, dishing up the meal and feeling she couldn't eat a single mouthful, was bewildered. For all the world, Pete was behaving as if he was the man of the house; sympathetic and understanding, but showing a degree of masterfulness which she'd never seen before.

Uncertain whether to resent or welcome this new dominance, she put the dish of vegetables on the table and sat down opposite him.

They ate in silence for a while, with Anna's thoughts running in circles. At last, too upset
149

to eat, she laid her knife and fork on the barely touched plate and spoke in a husky, uneven voice.

'Well, I'm surprised at you, Pete. I thought you were fond of Ros—but you don't seem to be bothered at all that she's gone off. Nowhere to sleep, no money for a meal, and that baby having to spend the night out of doors...'

Leaning across the table, she almost shouted the rest of her thoughts at him. 'You can't think so much of her, after all, if you're content to just let her go like this!'

Then, startled, she sat back in her chair. Pete's face had suddenly frozen into an agony of emotion, and his voice, when he answered, was tight with unreined feeling.

'You've got it all wrong, Mrs Hoskins. Dammit—I love her ... That's why I can let her go, why I had to let her go. Love has no strings, you see. But I don't think you understand that, do you?'

Time stood still as they held each other's eyes across the table and slowly, very gradually, Anna realised the truth.

Real love, as Pete had just proclaimed, had no strings attached to it. Whatever you gave with love was given freely, with no prospect of anything being returned. And so, because he loved Ros so dearly, Pete had let her go, not knowing if she would choose to come back to him.

The fact that he was missing her, worrying

150

about her, and tortured by the uncertainty of ever seeing her again, was just a part of accepting that love.

All the pent-up emotion inside Anna began to subside. If only she had realised earlier what living was all about, she could have spared herself so much. Still looking at Pete, she smiled, and put her hand out to touch his as it lay on the table.

'Thank you,' she said very quietly, and with utmost sincerity. 'You've made it all right. I do understand now. And I won't fuss any more. I'll just—just go on loving Ros—and Tom— and wait to see what happens.'

Pete's set expression relaxed into deep relief. He nodded and moved his hand to press hers warmly. He didn't speak, but Anna knew that they understood each other a little better now.

She took a deep breath, looked down at her untouched plate, and then back at him. There was a cheerier note in her voice, and the beginning of a twinkle in her eye when she spoke again.

'Do you know, I believe I could actually eat something, after all! Seems a pity to waste a good meal, doesn't it?'

Five minutes later the telephone rang. Anna's knife and fork clattered on to the plate as she ran into the hall, and for a moment she felt the return of that knot of nerves as it came to her that it might be Ros.

But it was Keith, his clipped voice becoming

151

sharp and edgy as she tried to explain Ros's absence. 'Gone? Gone where? She never told me. Did she leave an address?'

When she could get a word in, Anna tried to pacify him. 'No, I don't know where she is, Keith, but—'

'Good grief, you mean you let her go, just like that? And the baby? Not knowing where they were going? Well, you are a let-down and no mistake, Mrs Hoskins—I thought you were all set to look after them for me, see they were OK.'

Anna cut in very sharply, stung by the rebuke. 'You don't understand, Keith. I tried to stop her—her mother tried as well, but—'

'Her mother?' His voice swelled in a crescendo of sarcasm. 'What's she got to do with it?' He was shouting down the phone with a force that made Anna's eardrums vibrate.

She held the receiver at arm's length and waited until the metallic voice quietened, and said crossly, 'Are you still there? Haven't been cut off, have we?'

'I'm here, but I don't intend to talk any more until you calm down a bit, Keith. Just try to understand that Ros has gone off to sort out her feelings and her plans for the future.'

'Her future's with me! She knows that. We'd got it all planned.' he was yelling again, and Anna shook her head helplessly as the tirade continued: 'Going into the holiday flat, weren't we? And me with all my contacts organised.

What's she up to then, ditching me like this?'

Pete came to Anna's side, giving her his grave smile as he said firmly, 'I'll take the phone, Mrs Hoskins. No need for you to have to cope with this layabout on top of everything else.'

She handed over the receiver, but stood listening to the conversation that followed, as Pete said, in a very unfriendly tone, 'Pete Lazenby here. Stop shouting and let's get down to facts, shall we? Ros and Tom are off on their own for a couple of days. No need to get so worked up. After all, it's not as if she'd definitely said she'd wait for you, is it?'

There was a heavy, prolonged pause. Anna held her breath and stared as Pete raised a dark eyebrow in anticipation of Keith's reply. When it came it was loud and clear, words spitting down the wires with furious enmity; no doubt about it, Keith was in a proper state.

'Just who do you think you are, speaking to me like that? I'm the one who's going to help Ros sort out her problems. I certainly don't need you to tell me how to do it.'

'OK, OK,' Pete frowned. 'Let's forget that bit. The fact remains that Ros isn't dashing into marriage with you, mate. Not yet. She may do, later on, but—'

Anna looked at Pete and saw the anger spread across his face as he said the last words, and her admiration for him grew. She knew now, if she hadn't realised it earlier, that whatever Ros's ultimate decision, Pete would abide by it.

Fleetingly, she wondered whether Keith, in turn, possessed the same strength of character to enable him to take it in the same way.

But her thoughts were thrown into oblivion as Keith's voice came crashing down the line, making even Pete flinch beneath the fury of mounting rage and frustration. 'She may do? Hell, of course she will! You're not actually suggesting she might turn me down for you, are you? That's a good one!' But he wasn't laughing and the flow of words continued unabated.

'You're crazy! What would an intelligent, lovely girl like Ros want with a countrified idiot like you? Trust you to let her run off—you must be as weak as you are stupid. Well, I bet I know where she's gone, and I'll tell you this—I'm gonna find her and bring her back. And then it'll be just Ros and Tom and me. So go back to your fields and leave us alone.'

The line went dead and, as the dialling tone sounded, Pete slowly replaced the receiver, looking wryly at Anna as he did so.

'Got a very loud voice, has Keith Turner,' he commented flatly. Then he smiled into Anna's anguished eyes. 'I know how he must feel— reckon I felt the same when I knew she was going, at first. But I've had time to think. He hasn't.'

He hesitated and Anna said hotly, 'That's

very understanding of you—he said some awful things. He hardly deserves to be forgiven.'

Pete sighed and walked away towards the kitchen. In the doorway he turned sharply, looked back as if he wanted to say something, but just scowled—an unusual expression for Pete. Anna felt more confused than ever.

'Come and finish your tea, Mrs Hoskins.' Then the scowl was gone and again the good humour was back on his face.

But the day's traumatic events had taken their toll on Anna's stamina. Wearily, she shook her head.

'I don't want anything else. I think I'll go and sit down.'

'Right. I'll bring you a coffee.'

She heard him clearing the table as she sank down into her usual chair in the living-room, and was grateful for his presence in the house. Had she been quite alone, it would all have been too much to bear.

Then, out of the jumble of her thoughts, a name and a face suddenly emerged, bringing with them a feeling of comfort and reassurance.

'Freddie!' She had almost forgotten him. Oh, what a blessed relief to know that there was, after all, someone of her own age and generation she could turn to.

When Pete had finally said good night, telling her not to worry and that he was sure things would work out for the best, Anna drained the coffee he had brought her. She sat on in the gathering dusk for a while until she felt sufficiently rested to make the next move.

Then, pulling on a jacket and locking up the house behind her, she walked down the twilit lane. She felt increasingly content in the knowledge that Freddie would be glad to see her, and that he would understand her need of him at this uncertain and difficult moment in her life.

CHAPTER EIGHT

The walk down the empty country lane helped to restore Anna's downcast spirits. Honeysuckle gleamed, pale and fragrant in the dusk, and a thrush sang its mellow evening song, filling the world with tranquility.

Freddie's garden was, as usual, neglected and overgrown, but despite her disapproval, Anna noted how a jungle of flowers flaunted their colours, despite the weeds that tried to smother them. She wondered, momentarily, at the energy and persistence of nature, and then acknowledged wryly that people also needed those same attributes, if they were to overcome their problems.

She knocked gently at Freddie's door, smiling, ready to greet him as the true friend

156

she knew him to be. But he stared at her aghast as he opened the door, and she had an instinctive feeling that she wasn't welcome. But, the next minute, his surprise slid into the familiar wide grin, and he took her hand to lead her into the living-room.

'Come along! Just in time to help me choose the right package tour for my holiday! Sorry about the mess—push those brochures off the couch, will you, Anna? Those are the ones I've just been looking at ... that's it, sit down.

'Now...' He picked up another, garishly-coloured leaflet and brandished it under her nose. 'Take a look at this. What do you think, eh? Rather fancy it, I must say—'

Anna's problems were immediately submerged under the handful of advertising matter that he dumped on her lap.

'The price is right in this one, and it seems less full of concrete-block hotels. There are chalets with gardens and that sort of thing—much more my line, don't you think?'

His eyes sought hers, full of anticipation, and Anna quelled the small niggle of hurt that was rising inside her. Of course he was only thinking of his holiday and not of her; this was a dream about to come true and it would be despicable if she didn't try to share his obvious pleasure.

So, attentively, she read all the details, putting herself in his shoes and realising just how attractive the holiday was. The brochure

157

depicted small, wooden, thatched chalets, spaced out in beautifully-kept, colourful gardens and woodland, each building containing its own shower, bedroom and sitting-room, meals being provided in the huge, airy hall of the hotel around which the wooded gardens stretched.

There was a view of a silver-gilt beach not far away, where an unbelievably blue-green sea gently lapped, and pictures of the nearby city. Freddie's finger pointed excitedly to the attractions listed in the brochure.

'You see! Art galleries, museums, theatre, folk dancing, trips to outlying villages— everything I need; all that local colour. Oh, I'll be able to paint there...'

Watching, Anna saw his unremarkable face become almost handsome as enthusiasm and happiness grew. Gently she said, 'Of course you will.' Something deeply felt made her add, almost wistfully, 'You won't be lonely—on your own?'

Freddie's grin faded. Very simply he replied, 'My dear, I've been on my own ever since I can remember. I've learned to live with loneliness.'

As if rebuked, Anna bowed her head. 'Yes,' she murmured humbly. 'I know.'

For a long moment they looked at the pictures in silence. Then a small, hardly-heard sound made Anna blink. 'What was that?'

Freddie's eyes grew wary for a second. 'I didn't hear anything.'

'It sounded like someone in the kitchen. Or the passage. A door shutting, I thought...' She looked about her curiously, but Freddie was already burbling on again about his proposed holiday.

'No, you must have imagined it, old girl. Now—do you think I should settle for this one, eh? I'll get it all booked up tomorrow when I go into town. Have to find my passport, too. Where on earth could I have put it? Haven't used it for so long...'

He got up and began searching the drawers of his desk, and Anna sat back on the sagging couch, not quite sure whether to be amused or to feel neglected.

As if he felt the intensity of her thoughts, Freddie suddenly slammed shut the last drawer and turned to look at her thoughtfully.

'Sorry, love! Going on about myself, as usual. And you coming all this way down to see me. Anything wrong, Anna?'

It took a moment or two for her to adjust the thoughts milling around in her overwrought mind. When at last she began to speak, her voice was uneven and low, as the overpowering emotions once again threatened to swamp her.

'It's Ros, Freddie—Ros and Tom. She walked out this afternoon, wouldn't say where she was going. She's got no money, and ... and ... Oh, I'm so worried, I don't know what to do! Help me, Freddie—please...'

Her hands flew to cover her face as the tears

welled in her eyes, but not before she saw him staring at her across the room. She recognised instant understanding and compassion, but there was something else in his expression that didn't ring true. A holding back of some sort, a sense of disapproval, almost.

And yet, as he sat down heavily beside her, putting a hand on her shoulder, she knew he felt almost as wretched and torn apart as she did.

'Don't cry, Anna. Try not to worry. Ros is a sensible kid. She won't come to any harm, I'm sure. And she's not going to do anything silly that would harm her precious Tom, you know. Come on, cheer up.'

He patted her shoulder and then added very firmly, in a most un-Freddie-like way, 'Let's have a drink, eh? A little drop of brandy to make you feel better. Then I'll take you home. A good night's sleep is what you need. You'll feel fine in the morning.'

Was that all the comfort he could offer? Anna's pride forced the tears to dry up. She lifted her head, mopped her eyes, and said quietly, 'Yes, of course. You're right. I should never have come troubling you. And at this time of night, too. Not when you're so busy.'

The words, slightly sharp, died on her lips as Freddie's hands abruptly folded around her own, forcing her to look at him and meet the accusation in his suddenly-all-too-perceptive eyes.

160

'Don't be like that, Anna. You make it sound as if I don't care—which isn't true. I care very deeply about whatever happens in your life. And you know that. But the best advice I can give right now is to let the future look after itself.

'You must trust Ros to work out her own problems, you know. After all, we must all cope with our own lives. No one else can really help when it comes down to brass tacks—don't you agree?'

Helpless at the force of his words, quietly spoken as they were, Anna could only sit there and reflect. After a moment, Freddie smiled at her, reverting to the casual man she'd always known.

'I'll go and get that drink—sermon's over for today. But'—just for a second his smile died—'I think we both needed that little speech, don't you?'

The brandy brought new life to Anna's flagging mind. Freddie sat down beside her again, turning the glass slowly in his large, capable hands. She found his presence comforting now, no longer irritating as it used to be, and the unexpected advice he'd given her grew in sense and practicality as she thought back over it.

Looking at him, she found she was discovering facets she had never noticed before. Freddie was actually a thinking man, as well as being an artist, it seemed.

161

Perhaps she'd never encouraged him to speak his mind until now. She'd always been the one to call the tune, as it were, preferring him to follow in her footsteps, rather than allow him to have a say in things.

Now she discovered, she was intrigued with this new Freddie. What, for instance, did he think of the way she had treated Ray? Did he share her confusion over Keith? Would he ever agree with her inclination to one day allow Pete to take a bigger part in the running of Greenways?

Anna suddenly longed to share her problems with Freddie. And yet she had no right to do so. The fact that she'd kept him at a distance for so long, despite his obvious fondness for her, had surely closed the door to any deeper relationship between them now.

*   *   *

Again, everything had been her fault. She stared tragically over the rim of the brandy glass and felt her defences dissolve as all the problems abruptly joined forces on her.

'Oh, Freddie! I don't know how I can go on...' With shaking hands she replaced the glass on the table at her side, and met his anxious gaze. 'I'm so lonely, Freddie, I realise it, at last. Everyone else has something important to do, someone else to live for, or plan for ... and I—'

She gulped noisily, hating the surge of self-pity that had swamped her. 'And I haven't got anything, or anyone.'

Silence greeted her outburst, and her shame at having allowed it to overflow so indulgently made her turn away from Freddie's understanding eyes.

'It's all my own fault,' she muttered, finding a handkerchief and wiping her eyes briskly. 'I've learned a lot about myself during the last few weeks, I can tell you. I know I've been too immersed in my own affairs to think of other people and their feelings. Why, I even thought...'

She managed to laugh, an ironic, hurtful laugh. 'I thought I was self-sufficient, you see, not needing anyone else in my life. But I know now that I do need others. And suddenly I'm so alone.'

Freddie's hands found hers again. 'No, my dear, that's not true.' There was a fresh strength in his quiet voice that made her turn towards him, wondering. 'You're not alone, Anna. All of us loved you and tried to do what we could for you, but you weren't always ready to accept us.'

She saw his eyes abruptly flare with wry amusement, making him more like the old free and easy Freddie she had dismissed so peremptorily in the past.

'Until now,' he added slowly.

The laughter died, and a sternness slid across

163

his face. 'It's been a hard lesson, old girl. I know it has. But one that was necessary. We all need somebody to turn to.'

Anna thought for a long, silent moment. Then, as the unhappiness raging within slowly subsided, she was able to nod agreement and smile, meeting his direct and honest gaze with a new-found serenity.

'Thanks, Freddie,' she said huskily. 'You've said exactly what I needed to hear. It's good to have you as a friend.' Leaning over, she kissed his cheek, marvelling at the pleasure the gesture gave her.

Friendship should be openly exchanged and appreciated, she thought with a sudden stab of perception, and then was completely taken aback as Freddie's arms came warmly around her, his lips finding hers in a kiss that began in friendship, but continued with growing passion.

Breathless, she pulled herself away at last, unsure of how to cope with the feelings he had stirred in her.

Freddie's eyes held the old twinkle of good humour, as he released her. 'Nothing like a show of genuine fondness to make the world seem a better place. Love makes the world go round. Isn't that what they say? Now, don't look like that, my dear. Maybe I should have kissed you a long time ago. If I had, you wouldn't be going on about being lonely, would you?'

She could only return the smile. Freddie's hands were still holding hers and her lips obstinately savoured the pleasure of his kiss. After a moment's hesitation, she joined his spontaneous laughter and knew their relationship had taken a very definite step forward.

Getting to her feet, she pulled him up beside her, feeling suddenly restored to sanity and good humour.

'I wish—I mean, if only...' But words couldn't interpret her deep feelings. Speechless, she just went on smiling, meeting his eyes with a new and welcome frankness. She wanted desperately to let him see into her heart, to tell him of the regret and guilt that hid there; but also to free the new-found flowering of strength and affection.

After a moment, Freddie nodded and patted her hand. 'I know, Anna. Believe me, I do understand.' He led her towards the hall and she followed obediently, realising with a sense of wonder that words were unnecessary, for in some strange way he did, indeed, understand.

'I'll see you home, love.'

Anna shivered as the cool night air bit into her flesh, but Freddie's arm linked with hers as they walked down the lane and up the track to Greenways. By the time they reached the farmhouse she was glowing with warmth and well-being.

'I won't come in. Must get back...' For a

second a wary expression crossed his face, and then he added quickly, 'All that mess needs sorting out if I'm to book my holiday tomorrow.'

Anna's heart sank. She had only just discovered the depth of her feelings for him and the realisation that soon he would be going away was hard to accept. But she kept her smile in place. Lesson one, she thought wryly, never try to manipulate the people you love.

'How long are you going for?' she asked calmly.

'Three weeks this time.'

'You mean you'll go again?'

Freddie fidgeted uneasily. 'Well, if Keith goes on selling my pictures, I did just have the idea that I might pack up and go for good.'

He stared at Anna and she felt the unspoken accusation like a physical pain. 'I mean, there's no reason for me to stay. And if I've got a good market, I could paint even better out there than here. It's the light, you see—and the atmosphere...'

'Yes, of course.'

Silence touched them then. Anna sighed and felt herself stiffen.

'I think I'll go in. Thanks for bringing me home.'

'My pleasure, Anna.'

There was a moment's embarrassed hesitation and their hands brushed aimlessly. Anna opened the door with relief.

166

'Good night, Freddie.'

'Good night, love.'

She went to bed in the empty, creaking house with the memory of his questioning eyes filling her weary mind. Confusion came, deeper than before, and as she resolutely tried to settle into sleep, the matter of Freddie's love and of her own emerging feeling for him flew relentlessly around her mind like a trapped bird in a cage.

He loved her; yet he was going away. It seemed up to her, then, to take the next step, but that would mean facing her own depth of feeling and committing herself to a declaration of love. And she didn't think she could do that. Not yet. Perhaps not ever.

Next morning she got up earlier than usual, thankful to have tasks awaiting her. Fruit to pick, vegetables to harvest and pack, arrangements to be made for entries for the vegetable show at the week-end.

Thinking of this, Anna was reminded again of the disappearance of the ruby brooch and she discovered with surprise that she no longer suspected Keith of having taken it.

An opportunist he might be, but a common thief, no. With her awareness now painfully honed to a keener focus, she knew Keith for what he was and, despite his rather childish, immature ways, liked him.

For beneath his irritating habits and manner, she knew there was a rock-hard foundation of love for Ros and the baby. The

167

knowledge, though, did little to help her aching anxiety, for she could so well identify with Ros's inability to choose between Keith and Pete.

Pete—now, there was another man with strength. And he had a selflessness that Keith would never understand.

Anna went out to the vegetable field, shouting a cheerful good morning to Pete on the way. He straightened up from the row of peas he was stripping and looked at her with questioning eyes.

'Any news, Mrs Hoskins?'

Something inside her seemed to well over. So Pete had had a bad night, too, alone with his fears and emotions. Why had she never realised before that the world was full of unhappy, anxious people, besides herself?

Warmly, she forced a smile. 'Not yet, Pete. But I'm sure we'll hear something soon. Ros won't leave us too long without a word—she knows we're all worried about her.'

'Yes.' He looked at her curiously, and she read his expression correctly, smiling back a little bitterly as self-knowledge hit her yet again.

'I've been a fool, Pete,' she acknowledged bluntly. 'Thinking of myself all the time. What you said yesterday—about love having no strings attached—really made me see how badly I've treated everyone in the past. You, too.'

168

'Me?'

'Oh, yes. Making use of you. Not really caring about how you lived, or felt. Well, I know better now.'

He held her eyes and nodded sagely. 'I'm glad. You'll be all the happier for knowing.'

'Yes.'

For that moment they seemed very close. And once again Anna wished that he had been her son. Yesterday she might have clung to that and, in this new, shared intimacy, have tied him to her with the gentle pull of demanding affection. But now she knew differently.

So she straightened her shoulders, looking at the lush growth of the pea rows and said pleasantly, 'Are they yielding well? Do you think I might find a winner for the show on Saturday?'

She saw Pete's face clear as he returned her smile. 'They're really good this year. And, yes—I'll keep my eyes open for some likely entries. Look...'

He picked a long, fat pod hanging close by and split it open with his fingernails. 'One, two, three...'

'Nine!' Anna finished exultantly. 'Find some more like this and we'll stand a chance, I shouldn't wonder. I'd like to think that Greenways could bring home a trophy this year.' She looked at Pete squarely. 'Ray would have been thrilled. I want to win one for him.'

Pete didn't answer, simply nodding as he

bent again to the interminable task of stripping the long, thick rows. But Anna knew that he understood and approved her new attitude of mind. The knowledge helped her as she plodded bravely on through the long hot day, refusing to allow herself to worry about Ros and Tom.

*   *   *

She needed all her strength and determination later that afternoon when, unannounced, Keith appeared at the back door, anger showing in his face as he spoke rather abruptly to her.

'That damned road gets longer each time I come. Well, Mrs Hoskins, any news? I was going to phone from the station before I left town, but the train pulled out as I got there—'

He strode restlessly around the kitchen and Anna's hands shook as she filled the kettle. 'Nothing, Keith, I haven't heard any more, I'm afraid.'

He halted, inches from her, staring into her eyes with barely subdued fury. 'But that's crazy! You must have some idea where she went? Where did you look for her?'

'I—I didn't look anywhere.' She turned away from his unbelieving gaze, realising bleakly that this was going to be harder than she'd feared. 'Ros needed—needs—to be on her own,' she said firmly. 'She has a big

170

decision to make.'

He cut across her quiet words with a fierce intensity that frightened Anna. 'Rubbish! Ros and I had already decided what to do. There was no need for her to go off like this. Hell, why didn't you stop her, Mrs Hoskins? You've let me down! I thought I could rely on you to look after them, but it seems I was wrong.'

Yanking a chair over, he collapsed on to it, fingers drumming the table in front of him. Anna tried to push down the resentment that rose so quickly and went to make some tea.

He had no right to say such things. He was barely more than a stranger, a young man who, in the kindness of her heart, she'd taken into her home. Her anger grew and words erupted suddenly, without further thought, as she turned on him, resentment hot and punishing as it forced itself out.

'Don't you dare speak to me like that! You're a fine one to talk about letting anyone down ... you, the father of that gorgeous baby, leaving Ros unsupported and alone when she was pregnant and afraid. Oh, yes, Keith Turner, if I've been selfish then you've been equally so. And I don't blame Ros for wanting to get away from both of us!'

Clearly, Keith was stunned into silence by her bitter words.

Anna slammed a mug of tea on the table, adding fiercely, 'Now, drink this and then get out. I can't do with you here, all temper and

171

rudeness. I've got enough on my mind without you as well.

'Go and look for Ros if you must, but don't count on her wanting to marry you. After all, you let her down once; if I was Ros I'd want someone more reliable than you as a husband!'

They glared at each other in a silence that held more meaning than any words could convey. As Anna turned away, Keith reached out to spoon sugar into his tea. If Anna had been looking at him, she would have seen an expression of surprised awareness slide across his outraged face. But she had heard Pete's step in the yard, and was staring expectantly across the room.

Any minute now, she thought wearily, another confrontation, another row. I can't bear it.

But when Pete came in he was obviously in control and in no mood for baiting Keith. 'So you're back. Thought you would be. Mrs Hoskins told you we haven't heard from Ros?'

Keith nodded briefly and drank his tea, avoiding Pete's stare.

Pete added, 'I wouldn't mind betting we hear soon.'

Keith looked up to say sharply, 'And what makes you so sure about that?' His sarcastic words made Anna wince. 'Do you know something we don't?' He glared at Pete. 'So everything's under control, eh?' Fiercely, he got to his feet and swung across the room until he stood, threateningly, in front of Pete.

Anna watched in weary dismay. Pete now seemed as furious as Keith. But she lacked the stamina to part them.

Coldly, she turned away and went into the hall. If they wanted to fight, let them. Just as she had had to sort out her own problems, so they must sort out theirs.

Their enraged voices intruded noisily into her thoughts, Pete's voice mounting with anger. 'Shut up, will you, Keith! the trouble with you is that you haven't got any idea how other people think or feel—as long as everything's OK for you, you don't care about anyone else. Well, Ros couldn't take that any more.'

And Keith, cutting in stridently, 'And how do you know that? Going behind my back and chatting her up, I suppose—you creep! By God, I'll teach you to take my girl away from me.'

Anna closed her eyes in desperation and waited for the sound of warfare that such words must surely bring about. But no— amazingly, Pete had regained enough control to avert the threat of violence. His laughter rang out, forcing Anna's eyes to open, silencing Keith's hostile overtures.

'Pack it in, mate—we shouldn't be fighting! After all, we're on the same side, aren't we? We both want what's best for Ros and Tom, don't we?'

Silence. Anna held her breath, not knowing what to expect next. She was certainly unprepared for Keith's next words, spoken in a slower, more subdued tone. 'OK. So what do we do?'

She could have flown back into the kitchen and hugged them both. But instinct told her she wasn't needed. The two men must take the next step, whatever it might be.

*   *   *

In the hall, she tidied telephone books and rearranged the flowers on the table beneath the mirror, intent on hearing what was being planned.

Pete sounded hesitant. 'You said yesterday that you had an idea where Ros might have gone?'

'Yeah. Well, I was wrong.'

'But where, or who, could she have gone to?'

Keith growled frustratedly. 'Freddie, that's who. Just had an idea she might have gone there. I phoned him last night. But he said no. Of course, he could have been covering up...'

Anna stiffened. Ros, at Freddie's? Suddenly she remembered the noise of a door shutting; Freddie's wary expression; the way he'd changed the subject so quickly.

Dismay filled her. Freddie telling her lies while knowing she was worried out of her wits? Keeping Ros's safety from her? Oh, it just wasn't possible. Not Freddie...

The voices slid back into her disturbed mind. 'So that's one idea out of the window. Well, I'm sure she'll let us know when she's ready to come back.'

Keith grunted. 'If she comes back.'

'And if she doesn't ... well, that means we're both in the doghouse.'

Anna couldn't stand the suspense any longer. She went to the kitchen doorway and stared at them. Keith was striding up and down the room.

He shot a venomous look at Pete, who stood, impassive, by the fireplace. 'If that's so, you can make your own arrangements. Me, I won't accept it. Good grief, I love the girl.'

'And so do I.'

Abruptly, Keith halted to stare incredulously across the room and Anna saw the battened-down rage suddenly break free. He glared at Pete.

'Well, that's just too bad, mate! Because I'm going to find her, and take her away—from you and this god-forsaken place. From—'

'From me, Keith?' Impulsively Anna went into the kitchen and confronted him. Startled, he couldn't answer, and she went on. 'If Ros goes willingly with you, then I've nothing more to say. But, please—'

Suddenly desperate, she touched his arm and lowered her voice. 'Oh, please, Keith, don't do anything rash. Find her if you must.

Talk to her. But think about her happiness, as well as your own. I beg you, Keith—let it be what Ros wants.'

Keith stared down at her hand as it gripped his arm, an expression of wonder on his face. Then he met her eyes and she realised she had touched something in his heart. A small surge of hope began to lighten her misery.

Keith narrowed his eyes and said, more quietly, 'I'm sorry I said bad things to you just now, Mrs Hoskins. I didn't realise how you felt about Ros.'

Then the old cockiness slowly returned. He patted her hand as it still clutched at his arm, and grinned almost bouncily. 'OK, OK! I get the message. So I won't do the heavy husband bit. Just find her and get her to contact you. Let her be till she's made up her mind.'

The grin grew in confidence. 'The silly fool,' he added affectionately. Then, surprising Anna still more, he bent and brushed a rough kiss across her cheek. 'I'll be on my way then...'

With her mouth open, she watched him turn back to pick up his bag from the floor, hardly pausing to glance at Pete as he marched from the room.

'Cheers. I'll be in touch soon as I find her.'

Anna looked at Pete as the footsteps faded into the yard outside. 'Well!' she exploded with a wry grimace. 'Thank goodness that's over. What do you think he'll do?'

Pete silenced her, shaking his head and holding up a warning hand. 'Just a minute...' he said curtly. 'Yes ... I thought so.'

Bewildered, she could only stand and wait for enlightenment. It came almost immediately in the sound of the van starting up, and the screech of tyres as someone hurriedly and without care for gears or engines, drove out of the yard.

'He's taken the van!' She was catapulted into action, rushing to the door in time to see it disappear down the track in a cloud of dust. Furiously, she turned to Pete. 'You knew what he was going to do!'

Pete nodded, a touch of grim humour playing around his mouth. 'I saw him pick up the keys when he kissed you—they were on the dresser beside him.'

'Oh, really!' Anna wasn't sure whether she was angry or merely amused. 'The wretch! Why didn't you stop him then?'

Pete looked thoughtful. 'It'll be better to have transport to bring Ros home in—once he finds her, that is!'

Bring her home. At the words, Anna's mind immediately emptied of everything, save the dull ache of longing. To have Ros and Tom home again, at Greenways. She knew now that it was all she wanted.

She returned Pete's perceptive gaze, smiling a little mistily.

And then, suddenly, the telephone rang. For

177

a second, neither of them moved. Then Anna flew into the hall, holding the receiver to her ear with a feeling of sickening anticipation. Could it be Ros?

But it was Gilly, tearful and distraught. 'Anna? Oh, thank goodness you're there—it's Rosalind. I must talk to you about her...'

CHAPTER NINE

'Ros is here, Anna! She and Tom, here with me now!'

Gilly didn't seem to know whether to laugh or cry.

All the pent-up tension flew out of Anna's body at the welcome news and she sank into the chair beside the phone.

It was the peace after the storm, she thought, a brilliant shaft of sunlight refilling the dark and gloomy places of her personal world. Ros and the baby were safe. No longer did it hurt her that they had sought refuge with Gilly, the only thing that mattered was their well-being.

Then, after a moment, she remembered that Gilly was still on the line. Smiling through her own tears, she said warmly, 'Thank you for letting me know, Gilly—it's marvellous news. We were all so worried when Ros left.'

Gilly's voice grew calmer, a bubble of excitement making her sound younger and happier. 'She came late this afternoon, someone gave her a lift from the village, she said...'

Freddie, Anna thought, and this time without any recrimination. Bless you, Freddie. Aloud, she asked, 'Will she stay with you for a while? Until she decides what to do?'

'Yes. She's coming to the wedding—isn't it lovely? She and Tom will be here to see me marry Edward. Oh, Anna, I never thought she'd come back!'

Anna's face tightened and she wondered at the unfortunate choice of words.

But then Gilly laughed, a little flustered, and added, 'No, that's not what I meant to say. Ros is a mother herself now, and I can't expect to share her life as I used to. It's just wonderful that she's here, and that we're getting on so well, and—'

'—And that she came to you of her own free will, Gilly.'

Silence for a moment, as both women digested the truth of Anna's direct comment.

'I must go now,' Gilly said. 'There's so much to do with a baby in the house.' She paused. 'But you know all about that, don't you, Anna? After having Ros and Tom with you.'

'Yes. So much to do.'

After she had replaced the receiver, Anna sat on, lost in thought as the first immense relief and thankfulness gave way to a deeper examination of the situation.

Ros must have done some painful soul-searching. Now Anna realised how sensible Freddie had been to keep her in ignorance of having Ros and Tom in his spare room. Ros had badly needed that solitude and privacy—it might have been disastrous if Anna had forced her way in.

But, among these conflicting thoughts and images unreeling inside Anna's mind, one tiny pinprick of hurt grew deeper and more painful. Gilly hadn't said, Ros sends her love; not even a few words to apologise for the anxiety she had caused.

And so Anna was forced to face the unwelcome truth that she wasn't and never could be, as important to Ros as the girl was to her. She had had those first, wonderful moments of caring for Ros and Tom, of knowing that Ray would have been happy to see the little family secure at Greenways, but now life had moved on, and she must move with it.

Ros would be at Gilly's wedding, then wherever she settled would depend on how she saw her future. And I shall be alone here, once more ... Despite Anna's new awareness, and her determination to indulge in no more self-pity, the thought lingered.

Pete's voice startled her. 'Is she all right? I couldn't help hearing ... is something still wrong? I thought you'd come and tell me, but—'

180

Anna felt guilty. She rose, putting her hand on his arm as she answered quickly, 'No, no, everything's fine! I'm sorry, I was sitting there, thinking...' Firmly she pushed aside her own worries. 'Let's have a cup of tea, Pete—a funny sort of celebration, but I could do with one now!'

Her emotions had settled by the time they faced each other over the kitchen table, and she felt she could think constructively again. There were certainly several matters to consider.

'Let's forget Ros for the moment,' she said. 'Now, what am I going to do about Keith taking the van? I shall need it tomorrow for deliveries.'

'Were you thinking of reporting it to the police?'

The abrupt question startled her. 'No! I don't want to get the boy into trouble.'

Pete nodded, and looked amused. 'Not that he's a stranger to trouble, I reckon.'

They both smiled. 'I know what you mean.' Anna's voice grew firmer. 'But we have to try to find him. I want him to know that Ros is safe. Any ideas, Pete?'

'Not really. He could be anywhere in the district.' He looked thoughtful. 'What about the place they had in mind for his so-called business—a holiday flat, wasn't it? Do you know where it is?'

Anna shook her head, then a sudden thought came to her. 'Ros must know!'

'I'm not going to add to Ros's troubles,' Pete said. 'Imagine ringing her and saying Keith's run off somewhere with your van! No, Mrs Hoskins, we can forget that idea.'

'You're right. But we must do something.'

They sat in quiet companionship, not saying anything, until at last Pete got to his feet. 'I'll go and get ready for tea.'

The hint made Anna marshal her thoughts. 'Of course. Ready in half an hour, Pete.' Meeting his steady eyes, she heard her voice waver as she added, 'It's so wonderful to know that Ros and Tom are safe—I'd quite forgotten about tea.'

'It's OK, Mrs Hoskins—I know how you feel. Sort of—well, released from an awful nightmare.'

'Yes.'

She heard him walk rapidly across the yard, heading for his own home, and knew she had much to be thankful for. Ros and Tom safe with Gilly, and Pete's support here at Greenways. How lucky she was, indeed.

*   *   *

In the morning, her first thought was to look for the van, but it hadn't been returned overnight. An uneasy knot tightened inside her. What was Keith thinking of? Did he intend to come back when he was ready, full of the usual charm and apology? Or would he go on his way without ever realising how irresponsible his impulsive action had been?

Irritation began to stir as she hurried downstairs. Really, the boy was impossible, and she'd give him a piece of her mind when he did come back—if he came back. Her colour suddenly drained; what if he'd had an accident? He wasn't used to the old van's brakes and gears playing up.

Automatically setting out her breakfast, she shut her eyes and said aloud to the listening house, 'No, I won't think of such an awful thing. He's all right. Just—just looking for Ros...'

Then the unmistakable swish and scrunch of tyres halting in the yard outside made her run to the door, a smile already on her face and all thoughts of recrimination gone. He had come back!

'Keith—'

But it was a young, fair-haired policeman who stood on the step. He was good-looking, even with such an impersonal expression on his face. Steady eyes registered Anna's obvious shock and disappointment.

'Mrs Hoskins?'

'Yes.'

'Police Constable Mallory, Mrs Hoskins. I've come about a dark-green Ford van, registration number XTS three five six T, of which you're the owner.'

'Come in. It's—it's Keith, isn't it? Keith

183

Turner? Tell me quickly, please.'

'Sit down, Mrs Hoskins.'

She sank into a nearby chair while he watched her steadily, notebook open. Her heart was racing in anticipation. This gentle approach must mean something quite dreadful. When at last he began speaking, in his unemotional, country-burred voice, she knew he'd been right to break the news gently.

'Your van's been found on the B three eleven road into Broadwood, Mrs Hoskins, slewed on to the verge. Seems the driver failed to brake in time to avoid an articulated lorry coming round a corner in the opposite direction. The driver—' He paused to consult his notes.

Anna broke in quickly, 'Keith Turner was driving my van. He's—a friend. I let him borrow it.'

The lie came without thought or effort for, despite his many short-comings, Keith was a member of her small, valued family. Anxiously, Anna looked into the constable's blue eyes, but there was no trace of suspicion.

'Is he safe? Was he hurt? Or—or anything?' Just for a second her stomach churned. If something dreadful had happened to Keith, she would never forgive herself.

It seemed an interminable time before PC Mallory said, quite matter-of-factly, 'No, just roughed up a bit. He's being taken care of in the Cottage Hospital. Mrs Hoskins, can you definitely confirm that he had your permission to use the van?'

'Yes. He's a close friend of the family. Oh, yes, I said he could take it.'

'For what reason?'

Anna thought of telling him to mind his own business; why must she tell this impersonal young busybody about Ros and Keith? Her anger flared, but she was sensible enough to answer casually, 'A domestic matter. He was going to meet my—my stepdaughter, who's staying with her own mother.'

'I see.'

She held her breath, but no more questions followed. PC Mallory looked at her again. 'I'll need the car documents, please, Mrs Hoskins.'

As he left a few minutes later, he paused in the doorway to give her a last, keen stare. 'You're sure you don't wish to make charges against this Keith Turner?'

By now Anna was in control. She smiled at the suggestion. 'Good heavens, no. As I said, he's family, and I loaned him the van.'

'All right, Mrs Hoskins. Thanks for your help. Good day to you.'

As the police car moved slowly away from the back door, Anna, at the window, saw Pete emerge from his cottage and run over the yard, holding up a hand for the driver to stop. The two men spoke briefly, then Pete stood still for a moment as the car drove off, obviously thinking about the news he'd just heard.

Raising his head, he glanced across at the

185

house and Anna waved from the window. As if that had decided him, Pete briefly returned her wave, and then ran back to his home.

Anna went to the door, uncertain of what was happening. Why didn't he come for his breakfast? The answer, when it came, floored her. Pete reversed his rattly little Morris Minor out of the shed he used as a garage and drove it across to the house. Within speaking distance of Anna he wound down the window, shouting something which she couldn't hear properly because of the noise of the ancient car.

'What did you say?'

'Tell Ros ... back soon...' He waved, and urged the car out of the yard while, speechless, Anna watched him go, hardly believing that Pete, usually so staid, and sensible, could act so impulsively—thoughtlessly, too, leaving her here alone, with neither transport of her own or help for the tasks that waited.

Returning to the kitchen, though, she slowly realised that Pete had been right in going to break the news to Ros in person. She wouldn't want Ros to have a policeman arriving on Gilly's doorstep.

The answer to Anna's shock and anxiety was work; first she phoned the hospital and learned that Keith was as comfortable as a couple of broken ribs and severe bruising would allow him to be. Then she told Gilly what had happened, warning that official news would come at any moment and that, even now, Pete

186

was on his way to support Ros.

Finally, she turned to the chores outside—with Pete away, she knew she must work harder than usual.

*   *   *

The morning dragged on and, coming indoors for a forgotten invoice book halfway through preparing the soft fruit order, Anna was seized with an urgent need to contact Freddie. She couldn't bear it here on her own any more. She must swallow her stupid pride and forget how hurt she'd been about what he'd done. Impulsively, she picked up the phone.

'Freddie? It's Anna. Could you please come up and see me? So much has happened.' Her voice cracked. 'I need someone to talk to, Freddie...'

Within five minutes he was at her side, looking anxious and careworn. 'What is it, Anna? You sounded really upset.'

Her feelings erupted. Swinging around, she began shouting angrily, regretting the bitterness in her voice, but being unable to stop it.

'You lied to me! Ros was there the other night—in your spare room—all the time I was there. You said it was nothing when I heard that noise!'

Freddie sat down suddenly, looking defeated and apologetic. 'I know,' he admitted gruffly. 'But, you see, I'd given her my word. I said I wouldn't let anyone know she was there, not even you, love.'

'But you knew how worried I was!' Anna exploded. 'Surely you could have set my mind at ease? I'll never forgive you. Never.' She turned away, blinking hard.

There was a new, steely ring to Freddie's voice as he replied slowly but firmly, 'I'm sorry, my dear. But you're a mature woman, and she's so young. I thought it over, you see, and I came to the conclusion that her need was greater than yours.'

Anna looked at his dejected face and caught her breath in a bitter laugh of derision. 'And what do you know about my needs? An old bachelor like you...' Even as she spoke, she heard her own cruelty and hated herself for it. But the words had slipped out.

Freddie's face sagged and his eyes showed how she'd hurt him. 'There's no need to be like that, Anna.'

She could see he was trying to cover his dismay and pain, and wished with all her heart she could take back her words. Then the old Anna surfaced for a second, trying hard to excuse herself. Let him sulk, if he wanted to—it was true, wasn't it? He was a bachelor and so incapable of understanding how a married woman must feel...

But the image of his sad face struck deep and a moment later she spun around, words tumbling out in a torrent of apology and self-abuse.

'I'm sorry, Freddie! I'm bitter and hurt and worried. I want someone to blame, and you're here, so that's why I said it ... I'm so sorry...' Staring at him across the room, she saw how his eyes had brightened, noticed how he raised his head a little higher and leaned back, more relaxed, against the kitchen dresser.

She waited for the good-humoured, forgiving smile to return, as it had always done in the past, and then went on waiting, while Freddie merely returned her stare.

Slowly and grudgingly, she realised that he wasn't going to brush off the unpleasant little scene; he was expecting her to make the next move. She took it without further thought, for this was a new, stronger, more respected Freddie who stood so silently, waiting, and she knew she deserved this moment of honest confrontation.

She walked towards him with a resigned expression and put a hand on his arm. 'Forgive me?' she pleaded, her voice uneven. 'I don't deserve it, but ... oh, Freddie, I need you. Don't turn away from me, not now—'

As the familiar smile lifted his lips, she sighed with relief and laid her cheek on his chest. It smelled faintly of paint and turpentine.

Anna wished she could stay forever like this, secure and oblivious to all her troubles, but

Freddie gently pushed her away from him.

'Well, we'd better make some plans.' He patted her shoulder and she raised her head to see his face. 'I understand, Anna. You've been under a lot of stress lately. Now, how can I help?'

Suddenly she remembered the missing van, Pete's absence, and Keith's accident. Words poured out as she related everything that had happened since she last saw Freddie.

'And how I'm going to get the fruit delivered in time today I can't imagine,' she gabbled finally.

'No problem,' Freddie said airily. 'We'll take it on our way to the hospital. Come on, now let's get moving, shall we?'

How easily problems worked out, Anna thought, when you had a strong man at your side; wryly she watched Freddie piling the boxes into the back of his old estate car. At the restaurant he helped unload them again and then returned to the car, smiling broadly.

'Reminds me of my early days as an errand boy,' he commented. 'Now, ten minutes and we'll be at the hospital.' They drove in silence until he turned into the car park.

Slowing down, he looked at Anna very shrewdly. 'Don't lay into young Keith for taking the van, love. He has enough on his mind—and, his conscience, I shouldn't wonder.'

Humbly, she knew he was talking sense.

190

'You're right. I'll keep that rotten temper of mine in check.'

*   *   *

Inside the busy little country hospital, Anna's heart beat faster as she prepared herself for yet another unpleasant confrontation, for she and Keith hadn't exactly parted on the best terms.

But once inside the small, airy ward, she halted abruptly, for Pete was sitting beside Keith's bed, the two men conversing amiably and Keith, for all his bruised face and pallor, looking remarkably relaxed as he recognised her.

Pete stood up, uncertainly. 'Mrs Hoskins, come and sit down.'

'I didn't expect to find you here!' Anna's quick retort slid out and immediately she felt Freddie's restraining hand on her arm.

'I told Ros I'd come and see how Keith was.' Pete seemed ill at ease and Anna decided to put him out of his misery.

She took the chair he'd just vacated and smiled briskly at the watchful Keith as she sat down. 'Well, Freddie and I decided to do just the same thing. Lucky for me he has a car, don't you think?' She glanced meaningfully at Pete.

'Mrs Hoskins, I'm sorry I just took off like that, without telling you, but—'

Anna could see exactly how remorseful he

191

felt. Her smile grew warmer and more gentle. 'It's all right, I understand. You wanted to reach Ros before the police got there—well, thanks for that, Pete.'

Keith's voice was as chirpy as ever as he broke the short silence. 'OK, so that's all cleared up and everyone's happy again. So how about asking the poor wounded hero how he is? Good grief, I was hoping for a bit of sympathy.'

'Well, you won't get any from us!' Anna's voice was teasing.

'It's great to see you, Mrs Hoskins.' Keith flapped a listless arm in her direction. 'Good of you to come, all things considered.' The grin subsided and he looked at her more seriously. 'Reckon I'm in the doghouse for pinching your van, eh? Badly damaged, so the copper said. And I'm broke.'

Anna surprised herself by answering calmly, 'Never mind all that; the only really important thing is that you're safe and not too badly hurt.'

She watched Keith digest her unexpected words and realised that his customary edginess was merely a defence. In his own way he was as soft and vulnerable as Ros.

'Ros!' she exclaimed suddenly, turning to look at Pete. 'You saw her? Is she all right? And Tom?'

'They're both fine. Ros is a bit shattered by everything, of course, but her mum's being marvellous. She's going to bring Ros and Tom to visit Keith later on, when young Tom's had his sleep.'

'Thank goodness.' Anna breathed an enormous sigh of relief. The nightmare was behind her now, with only a few loose ends to tidy up.

As the men chatted between themselves, she sat back and began to wonder how she would manage without the van. Would her insurance cover the damage, and, if not, could she afford to have it repaired? And if Keith really was as broke as he'd said, how on earth did he expect to be able to support Ros and Tom when they set up home together? If they did...

Even as all these worries surfaced, she felt Freddie's hand on her shoulder. 'We'd better go, love. Reckon the lad's had enough excitement for the moment. Well, 'bye, Keith—and good luck, my boy.' He leaned over the bed, holding out his hand.

Keith took it thoughtfully, the movement making him wince with pain. 'Thanks, Freddie. Hell! How long do broken ribs take to mend? Can't see myself moving job lots around like this.'

Pete's deep voice was amused. 'Six weeks, mate, that's how long. I fell off the tractor a couple of years ago, so I know.'

'Trust you to do something like that,' Keith commented, but Anna saw how the two men grinned at each other without any rancour on

193

either side.

She rose. 'Good-bye, Keith, I hope you'll soon be on the mend.' At the door she looked back at him. 'Of course, I've no idea what your plans will be but—' She chose the next few words, with great care. 'But if things don't turn out as you expect, and you need somewhere to stay for a while, I'll be pleased to have you at Greenways.'

'Thanks,' Keith said quietly.

He looked pale and very young against the clinical white pillow, and Anna's emotions surged. He was, after all, just a young, simple lad who needed a second chance. Perhaps everything would work out all right, even now, if Ros said yes to him.

Freddie was smiling at her with approval, and she knew that her invitation to Keith had pleased him. He took her hand.

'Come on, Anna, home for lunch, eh?'

Pete's voice followed them into the corridor. 'I'm coming, too, Mrs Hoskins. Just want another quick word with Keith—'

Out in the car-park, Anna paused, feeling the sun on her face and sensing the beauty of the day, despite its traumas and worries. She smiled brightly at Freddie as he slipped into the seat beside her.

'Sunshine makes such a difference to life, doesn't it?' And then, the connection of ideas made her ask lightly, covering up the loneliness that came at the same time. 'Have you booked your holiday in the sun yet, Freddie? You'll love it in Florence...'

Freddie waited until he had negotiated the round-about on the outskirts of the village and was heading for home before he answered. 'Not yet. Thought it could wait a bit longer, actually.' His voice sounded too casual and he kept his eyes glued to the road ahead.

'But why? You were so keen the other night.' Anna felt confused. She could see no likely reason why he should change his mind now.

'M'mm, yes, but—well, you never know, do you? I mean, things crop up and then you have to make other arrangements.' He didn't quite explain himself and she could only shake her head wonderingly. Freddie's ways were strange indeed, but she knew better now than to argue with him.

*   *   *

Greenways, as always, welcomed her home. 'Stay and have a bite of bread and cheese with us,' she invited Freddie as he came in to the kitchen after her. Something about his answering glance forced her into foolish excuses. 'Pete will be here soon. He'll want to tell us all about Ros and Tom.'

Pete returned just as they had sat down, his little car chugging noisily into the yard and bringing Anna to her feet again. She went to the door to welcome him, for, stupidly

195

perhaps, she felt she must let him know at once that she harboured no resentment about his swift departure earlier.

'Come in, Pete, lunch is all ready.' Her eyes searched his face, and her smile faded as she instinctively sensed that there was still something wrong.

Pete looked at her bleakly. 'Thanks, Mrs Hoskins. But I'm not hungry.'

'Then you must have a coffee or something. Sit down and I'll put the kettle on. For heaven's sake, Pete, you look like a wet week-end!' She forced brightness into the foolish words and had the satisfaction of seeing a weak smile lift his sombre face.

Somehow she managed to keep a conversation going, with Freddie helping, and then at last saw Pete's expression change, and knew that the moment had come when he felt he could tell her about his worries.

'What is it, Pete? Do tell me . . .'

Freddie scraped back his chair. 'I'll leave you—'

'No!' Pete's voice was unexpectedly firm. He pushed aside his cup and looked first at Anna, then at Freddie. 'Don't go, Mr Freeman. We're all in this together, aren't we? The thing is . . .'

Anna waited while he paused, and felt a deep affection start to rise within her. She hadn't realised until now how important Pete's well-being was to her, and it hurt to see him so distressed. Silently, she laid her hand over his,

196

feeling the hard, calloused skin, and appreciating yet again all the help Pete had given her since Ray died.

As he felt her touch, Pete looked up, and his grim expression relaxed slightly. 'I have a confession to make, Mrs Hoskins. About your ruby brooch.'

Pete, a thief? Anna caught her breath.

'Oh, don't worry,' he said as he caught the look on her face. 'I didn't steal it. But I let you think Keith had done, when all the time I knew where it was.'

Gently, Freddie asked, 'Why did you do that, lad?'

Pete sighed as he answered. 'I suppose because I needed a weapon of some sort to use against him. You see, I thought that if Ros thought he'd taken it, then she wouldn't want any more to do with him, then she'd turn to me. Rotten, wasn't it? I know.'

Meeting Anna's eyes, he fished the brooch out of his pocket and pushed it over the table to her. 'Here's your brooch, Mrs Hoskins, safe and sound. You must have dropped it when you took that jumper out of the car after the show, remember?'

Anna nodded slowly and picked up the brooch. It was solid and reassuring in her fingers and she knew it would look spectacular worn against Ros's young, fresh beauty, where it belonged.

'I remember. So you found it, but didn't give
197

it back?'

'Reckon I just forgot. Put it in the pocket of my best trousers that I wore that day and didn't put them on again for months. I just forgot to bring it back to you. Then, when you said it was missing—well, I had this idea.' He shook his head. 'Never done anything like that before. I suppose you must think I'm pretty mean and calculating. You and Ros.'

He dropped his eyes and suddenly Anna was able to laugh at the whole ridiculous situation. He looked up, aghast at her unexpected reaction.

'You're as bad as Keith! What a pair! Both trying so hard to impress poor Ros. Oh, Pete, don't look so glum! All's well that ends well, you know. I'm delighted to have the brooch back, and no one but me will ever know about your wicked schemes!'

Abruptly she turned to look at Freddie, adding, quietly, 'I mean, no one but Freddie and me—and I'm sure he doesn't think too badly of you.'

Freddie's face lit up. He looked deep into Anna's eyes, and then glanced back at Pete, trying to make his voice sound casual.

'You can count on me, lad. Went through a bad patch, didn't you? Well, it's only human nature to act as you did, after all. Your secret's safe with me, Pete.'

'But it's not a secret,' Pete said determinedly. 'Ros knows. And Keith, too—I told him after

198

you left this morning.'

'Well, that was pretty noble of you. How did he take it, lad?'

'He thought it was hilarious,' Pete said wryly. 'But then he cursed me for making his ribs hurt...'

'And Ros?' Anna was curious.

Pete's face relaxed and a smile touched his lips. 'She said she never thought Keith had taken it, and it didn't matter that I'd pretended that he had.' Pete thought hard, then he smiled at Anna and shrugged. 'She understood,' he said simply.

For a long moment they sat in silence, thinking over all that had been said, then Pete got up, pausing as he pushed his chair under the table. 'But I knew I had to make things right with Keith—I felt so guilty, you see. So I told him I'd pay for the damage to the van.'

'Pete, you don't have to do that!'

'Yes, Mrs Hoskins. It's the least I can do. And I've asked Keith to come and stay with me when he leaves hospital, I mean, until Ros decides what she wants to do...' His voice tailed off uncertainly.

Anna felt a great admiration surge through her but Freddie said it all. 'Good for you, boy. You did the right thing.'

Pete's face brightened. 'Glad you think so. That's made me feel much better. You see, I realise Keith's not a bad guy really—he's got Ros's well-being at heart, even if he doesn't always show it.' Abruptly Pete turned and headed for the door. 'He might even make a reasonable husband, who knows?' he added as he disappeared into the yard.

Anna looked at Freddie, knowing she had tears in her eyes. He took her hand in his.

'A good lad,' he commented. 'A heart of gold in that boy. Ros'd be mad if she chose Keith instead of him. But she's got to make up her own mind, eh, love? No business of ours.'

Anna shook her head, content that Freddie had said ours. She was no longer on her own, it seemed, and it was a good feeling, whether it lasted or not. Wisdom grew as she watched him pile up the dirty dishes and take them to the sink. Live for today, she reminded herself. Enjoy this moment, and don't worry about what comes next.

*　　*　　*

During the afternoon Gilly phoned. She sounded bright and busy, and invited them all to come to supper. 'Bring Freddie, and Pete, too. Celebration time!' she said excitedly. 'Please come, Anna, Ros badly wants to see you.'

At those last few words Anna's happiness soared, and when on arriving at Gilly's house Ros met her on the steps and flew into her arms, her joy was complete.

'I've been so stupid—forgive me.' Ros

200

looked at her with Ray's warm smile and Anna could only nod and hug her tightly. 'It's all right,' she whispered. 'You're safe, you and Tom. Nothing else matters.'

Then Edward appeared, and the emotional reunion was over. After drinks in the sunlit garden room, they sat around the gleaming oak table in Gilly's elegant, mock-Tudor dining-room and ate fresh salmon and Ros's strawberry shortcake, and Anna knew it was an occasion to be cherished. Never mind what the future held for any of them —this was an unforgettable evening of shared happiness.

Later, when Ros explained that she planned to stay with Gilly until the wedding, a fortnight ahead, Anna felt no resentment. She knew that Ros would come to Greenways when she wanted to.

And how right she was! 'About the flower show,' Ros said tentatively, as they parted on the moonlit doorstep. 'I'd love to go in for the Cake Competition. Do you think I could come home for a few days? This week-end, isn't it?'

Home, Anna felt herself smile—she had never dared hope that Ros might think of Greenways as home. Somehow she pulled herself together and answered, a catch in her voice.

'Of course you can come, love. Yes, the competition is on Saturday. I'll get in my groceries on Friday. Let me know if you want anything special.'

The days sped by after that, with happiness replacing the dark clouds that Anna had experienced so recently. On Friday morning, Freddie drove Ros and Tom back from Gilly's, and at the same time Pete collected Keith from the hospital.

They all met in the yard, and if Anna had expected there to be any recrimination or awkwardness between Ros and Keith, she was disappointed. With Tom in her arms, Ros ran to Keith directly she saw him. They hugged warmly.

'Steady on, Ros,' Keith exploded, putting his hands up to protect his wounded chest in a comical gesture. 'The trouble is you don't know your own strength.'

Laughter spilled out and Anna saw how Ros hung on to Keith's arm as she led him towards the cottage, and how honest Pete's smile was when he paused at the front door to say hello.

She went indoors and left them all together, her head full of the sheer joy of having her little family home again, and for once at peace with one another.

They all came to supper, which turned into a memorable meal. The house was again full of noise and activity, and how young Tom ever managed to sleep through it, up in Ros's room, Anna never knew.

Ros seemed to be glowing with health and happiness, and Anna wondered briefly if her decision had been made. Would Ros tell them, perhaps, during the evening?

It was Pete who broke the news. Suddenly, he lifted his glass of wine and turned to Anna, at the head of the table. She held her breath. There was something fresh and wonderful shining in his eyes.

'I've asked Ros to marry me and she's said yes,' he burst out, and, in the silence that followed, looked at Ros, sitting by his side, with such impassioned joy that, as usual, Anna wanted to weep.

But she didn't. Instead, and with a calmness that surprised even herself, she raised her own glass and glanced round the table, as if asking them all to join her. Freddie did so at once. And, finally, Keith...

'Bless you both,' Anna said, and they drank the toast in silence.

Then, of course, followed the explanations, the plans, the reasons.

'We'll live here and Pete can still work on the smallholding,' Ros announced, looking at Anna pleadingly, as if she was afraid it might not be a welcome idea.

Pete added gently, 'That's if it's OK with you, Mrs Hoskins?'

'OK. It's wonderful!' Anna could hardly contain her happiness. Then she looked down the table at Keith's somewhat glum expression.

Keith stared back, understanding her concern. Suddenly he stuck out his chin determinedly and leaned across the table to look directly at Pete.

'Good luck, mate,' he said firmly. 'I reckon the best man won, eh? The last few days have taught me that you're not such a bad chap, after all. You'll look after them all right won't you?'

'You can bet your life I will, Keith.'

'And you'll come and see Tom whenever you want, Keith,' Ros said huskily. 'I'm glad you understand.'

He took her hand, giving it a gentle squeeze. 'Just make sure that my son knows who his real dad is, that's all. I wouldn't want him to forget me.'

Ros's gentle smile turned into laughter which spread around the table. Suddenly an idea which Anna had been turning over for a while came to mind.

'Pete,' she said urgently, 'I want you to be my partner in the business. Yes, really, I need someone to take some of the pressures off me.'

His amazed face brought a chuckle to Keith's lips. 'Yes, this old country bumpkin should be just the chap,' he joked. 'And if either of you want any help with business matters—well, I'm always at the end of a phone, remember.'

Amid the laughter Pete looked at Anna. 'I don't know what to say,' he said quietly. 'It's the most wonderful thing that could happen to me. Are you sure, Mrs Hoskins?'

Anna sighed delightedly. 'I'm sure, Pete.'

She smiled. 'And forget about calling me Mrs Hoskins—it's Anna from now. After all, we're going to be partners, aren't we?'

He held out his hand and she shook it, feeling the strength and warmth with the realisation that she had done the sensible thing.

'Partners,' she repeated, and they smiled at each other.

*   *   *

Freddie refused to let anyone help with the washing-up, except Anna. His forcefulness surprised her, but she allowed him to take charge of the great pile of dirty dishes and saucepans.

'I didn't know you liked washing-up,' she teased, and he looked over his shoulder with mock severity.

'I don't. But it's the only way I could get you on my own.'

She halted, a tea towel in her hands, for Freddie was looking at her very pointedly and his voice was firm and certain.

'What—what do you mean?' she asked.

He turned off the hot water and took her hands in his, tea towel and all. 'I mean that this is my chance to ask you to come to Florence with me. I love you very much, Anna, and I think you're fond of me, too. Let's try and make a go of it, eh?'

'Well...' Now everything slid into place,

205

and after a second's hesitation, she added a definite, 'Yes, I will!' It didn't matter that this hadn't been a formal proposal of marriage—maybe neither of them needed that much commitment, not yet. Time would tell.

Anna put her arms around Freddie, dropping the tea towel as she did so, and kissed him soundly. 'How badly I need a holiday,' she murmured. 'And being with you will make it a really happy one ... thanks, Freddie, dear, I'll come with you with the greatest pleasure in the world.'

After that, the large pile of washing-up was dealt within a flash as they discussed plans and shared dreams, both of them enjoying the thought of the new experience to come.

When Freddie had at last gone home, his loving eyes still fresh in her mind, and Ros, Pete, and Keith had all gone to bed, Anna sat on in the empty kitchen, reliving the evening.

How little she had guessed, after Ray's death, that she was entering a new world. Pain and hurt had been part of it, but now the love which had come to her through the pain had won through. The experiences of her earlier years had, unknown to her, grown into a new security and happiness. Going up to bed, Anna knew herself to blessed, and rejoiced.

Her last thought before drifting off to sleep was that Ray would be happy to know that in future Greenways would rest in the capable hands of his daughter and his grandson. And that Anna herself, either in Italy, or wherever her new relationship with Freddie dictated, would be always on hand to give loving and willing support.

In the morning she awoke with a start, knowing that something important was due to happen today—what could it be? Last night's memorable happenings still lingered, but suddenly she remembered.

The Flower Show!

Ros's cake; her own offerings of peas and cut flowers; Freddie's paintings on show—so much to do...

The mirror showed her face sparkling with energy and happiness. She ran downstairs and found Ros in the kitchen, feeding Tom. They smiled at each other happily.

'I'll get the breakfast ready,' Anna said rapidly, the smile never leaving her face. 'You get Tom dressed, and then Freddie can collect you. I'll come down later with Pete and...'

They looked at each other and began to laugh.

Another day had started and there was so much to do.

We hope you have enjoyed this Large Print book. Other Chivers Press or G.K. Hall & Co. Large Print books are available at your library or directly from the publishers.

For more information about current and forthcoming titles, please call or write, without obligation, to:

Chivers Press Limited
Windsor Bridge Road
Bath BA2 3AX
England
Tel. (01225) 335336

OR

G.K. Hall & Co.
P.O. Box 159
Thorndike, Maine 04986
USA
Tel. (800) 223–2336

All our Large Print titles are designed for easy reading, and all our books are made to last.